THE GUNSMITH

408

The Gold of Point Pinos

Books by J.R. Roberts
(Robert J. Randisi)

The Gunsmith series

Gunsmith Giant series

Lady Gunsmith series

Angel Eyes series

Tracker series

Mountain Jack Pike series

COMING SOON!
The Gunsmith
409 – Shot in the Back

For more information
visit: www.SpeakingVolumes.us

THE GUNSMITH

408

The Gold of Point Pinos

J.R. Roberts

SPEAKING VOLUMES, LLC
NAPLES, FLORIDA
2024

The Gold of Point Pinos

ISBN 979-8-89022-266-4

Chapter One

When Clint came to the beach he dismounted and led Eclipse out over the sand. The big Darley walked gingerly until he was fairly sure his footing was secure.

Clint stared out at the expanse of Monterey Bay. He had been to California many times before, but this was the furthest South he had ever come.

His intention had been to get away from the "old West" for a while. People had been telling him for years that the West was changing, wasn't what it used to be. They also said it didn't have a place for men like him, who lived by their guns. Those days were done.

Clint wasn't ready to be obsolete, but he was ready to take a break, and rather than travel to New York City or somewhere else on the "civilized" East coast, he made up his mind to go West. Once he got to San Francisco he'd been challenged right away, and after dispatching the challenger without killing him—through pure luck—he'd decided to head South.

Along the way someone had told him about the coast of Monterey, as well as the towns and cities in the area—most specifically Monterey itself, as well as a place called Pacific Grove.

He stood on the beach for a good fifteen minutes, with Eclipse pawing the sand every so often to indicate his mild displeasure.

"I know, I know," he said, "you want to be on more firm ground." He patted the horse's neck. "Just let me stand here and breathe this clean ocean air for a few more minutes and we'll be on our way."

Eclipse remained silent, but continued to paw at the loose sand.

"All right, all right," Clint said, "take it easy. We'll get going."

Rather than mounting Eclipse on the sand he walked the horse to more solid ground, then swung into the saddle.

"All right, big boy," he said, "let's head for Pacific Grove and see what we can fin—"

He was interrupted by the sound of voices. They seemed to be shouting.

"Help, help," someone was yelling. It sounded like a child's voice, an older child.

He heard someone else calling, "Get him, damn it!" that sounded older, like an adult. He stood in the saddle and looked around. He saw three men running on the beach, and they seemed to be pursuing a single, smaller individual.

He sat back down in his saddle.

"We should just head for Pacific Grove, right boy?" he asked. "Mind our own business? Stay out of trouble?"

Eclipse pawed the solid ground. Whatever Clint was going to decide, the Darley Arabian wanted him to do it fast.

At that moment he heard the voice shout, "Oh, help me!" again.

"Damn it!" he said. "Came all this way to mind our own—aw, come on, Eclipse. Let's go!"

***

Eclipse still didn't like the feel of his hooves on the sand of the beach, but at least this time he was running.

Clint had several options. Ride down the three men who were chasing the kid, or ride up to the kid and snatch him—or her—up. Since he didn't know who the men were, or how armed they were, he decided on the latter.

He rode up the beach with the running people ahead of him. As he rode past the three pursuers, he heard one of them shout, "Hey!"

He rode past them and quickly caught up to the running figure. When he came alongside and looked down he was surprised to find it was not a child, but a girl. She looked up at him, her eyes wide with fright.

"Do you need some help?" he asked.

"I—I can't—" she said, looking back over her shoulder. She looked back at him, obviously not sure who he was there to help. "Who are—"

"Come on," he said, reaching down. "I'll help you get away."

She was hesitant.

"Or you can keep running, and eventually they'll catch up to you."

Still hesitant. She looked back over her shoulder again, saw that her pursuers were even closer.

He shook his hand at her.

"Make up your mind."

She lunged wildly for his hand and missed. But he closed his hand around her forearm and pulled her up into the saddle behind him.

"Hold on tight!" he said.

Chapter Two

When they had left the three men behind, Clint reined in, reached behind him for the girl and lowered her to the ground. Then he dismounted and removed his canteen from the saddle.

"Here you go," he said, handing it to her.

"Thank you." She drank some water and handed it back, wiping her mouth with her sleeve. Her face was dirty, and beneath the dirt she looked sixteen or seventeen.

"You can rest here a while," he said, hanging the canteen back on the saddle, "maybe tell me what that was all about?"

She tightened her lips.

"Yeah, you're right," he said, "you don't have to tell me. All I did was give you a ride."

"I appreciate it."

"I'm glad to hear it," he said. "Is there someplace you'd like me to drop you?"

"No," she said, squinting against the sun, "I can make my way from here."

"What if those men catch up?"

"They won't," she said, "but if they do I'll outrun 'em."

"Like you were doing when I found you?"

"They surprised me."

"Uh-huh."

He mounted up.

"You got a name?"

"Billy."

"That's a boy's name."

"Billie," she said, "with an 'i' and an 'e'. That's a girl's name."

"Okay, Billie, with an 'i' and an 'e'," he said. "Good luck."

"Where are you headed?"

"Don't know for sure," he said. "Pacific Grove, I guess, and then maybe Monterey."

"In Pacific Grove," she said, "there's a rooming house on Clarke Street. If you wanna stay overnight, or a few days, go there. Tell Mrs. Evans you know me. She'll give ya good deal."

"Okay," he said, "I'll do that. Thanks, Billie."

"See ya."

She looked around, found a likely spot and sat down, presumably to rest. Or maybe she just didn't want him to know which way she was going to go after he left.

"Hey, Billie."

She looked up at him.

"Point to Pacific Grove."

She smiled and pointed.

"Thanks," he said, and rode in that direction.

***

Pacific Grove was a small town that looked like it was having growing pains. There were buildings in different stages of construction, and Clint could smell the newly sawed wood that was being used. They were also close enough to the beach for him to still smell the sea water.

He came to a small saloon and decided to stop for a beer before figuring out whether to stay overnight or move on. It was early afternoon, so there was still enough light to ride on if he wanted to.

The saloon was called the Beach Grove Saloon, which looked odd as hell to Clint's eye, but certainly fit right in with where he was. He dropped Eclipse's reins loosely over a hitching rail so that he'd look tied off even though he wasn't. If Eclipse ever moved from where Clint left him, it would be for a good reason. But there was no reason to tempt someone to take him by actually dropping his reins to the ground.

He entered the saloon, found it's fairly small interior about half full. The men drinking there in the early afternoon gave him a brief look, then went back to what they were doing.

He walked to the bar, where a tall, slender, young bartender greeted him with a smile.

"Help you, friend?" he asked.

"Beer," Clint said, "cold, if you've got it."

"Cold like ice, yes sir," the bartender said. "Coming up."

The bartender went for the beer and brought it back to Clint with the same smile still plastered on his face.

"Nice looking town," he said to the young man.

"Yes, sir," the bartender said, "and getting nicer. You just get here?"

"Just rode in."

"Thinking about staying a while?"

"Maybe," Clint said, after a sip of beer. "Got any good hotels?"

"Yes, sir, a couple, just up the street," the bartender said. "One's called the Beach House, and the other one's the Coral."

"Coral?"

"It's a shell you find on the beach."

"Ah," Clint said. "The town sure makes good use of the fact that the beach is nearby."

"Yes, sir," the bartender said, "lots of folks come here for the water."

"And the beer, I'll bet," Clint said. "It's very good."

"Thank you, sir. 'scuse me."

Another customer had walked in, and the man went to serve him.

Clint worked on the rest of his beer slowly, looking around. No one seemed to be paying any more attention to him.

"Another one?" the bartender asked, returning.

"No," Clint said, "I'll just finish this one."

"Lots of folks come here for the lighthouse, too."

"Lighthouse?"

"Yes," the man said, "the lighthouses were built about thirty or so years ago, to help ships negotiate the rocks as they enter and leave the bays, like Monterey Bay."

"I see."

"You should stay and have a look at Point Pinos."

"Point Pinos?"

"That's our lighthouse," the man said. "It's the southernmost of all the lighthouses."

"Sounds interesting."

"Take a look at the hotels," the bartender said. "And the town. And when you see the lighthouse, you'll see that it was worth staying."

Clint finished his beer and set the empty mug down on the bar.

"I'll have a look around," he said. "Thanks for the beer. What do I owe you?"

"On the house," the bartender said. "Come again."

Chapter Three

Clint left the saloon and instead of mounting up he walked for a few blocks, leading Eclipse behind him. He was greeted several times by people on the street with "Hello, friend," or "How are you?" and never found himself the object of so much as an arched eyebrow.

He passed both hotels the bartender had told him about. He didn't see a sheriff's office, but he did see a two story brick building with the words POLICE STATION on it. Across from the building was a new barn, housing the livery stable. He filed that away for future reference and decided to go and look for the rooming house the girl, Billie, had told him about.

***

After asking a man on the street for directions he found Clarke Street, and the rooming house. He left Eclipse at the front gate and walked to the door. His knock was answered by a handsome woman in a long, high-necked cotton dress, her honey colored hair pinned up on her head.

"Yes?"

"Are you Mrs. Evans?"

"I am."

"I was told you had rooms?"

She studied him for a moment with intense brown eyes, then folded her arms.

"And who told you that?"

"A girl named Billie."

She dropped her arms.

"Billie? Have you seen her today?"

"Yes," he said, "this morning."

"Where was she?"

"On a beach not far from here."

"What was she doing?"

"Well—"

"Wait," she said, "I'm sorry. Y-yes, I have rooms. Would you like one?"

"Yes, I would."

"For how long?"

"I'm not sure. A couple of days, maybe."

"All right," she said. "Come in, please."

She backed away and allowed him to enter.

"Would you please tell me what Billie was doing when you saw her?"

"Well . . . she was running away from three men."

"What?"

"On the beach," he said. "Three men were chasing her."

"But . . . why?"

"I don't know," he said. "I rode up and picked her up, rode her away from those men, but then she wanted to be on her own and wouldn't tell me why she was being chased."

"And you left her alone?"

"Well, Mrs. Evans, she knows her way around here better than I do. In fact, she pointed me to Pacific Grove and told me about you."

"And she was all right when you left her?"

"She was fine," Clint said.

"Not . . . frightened?"

"Not when I left her," Clint said. "While she was being chased, yes. She was calling for help. I heard her, which is how I found her. She looked scared when I grabbed her, but she was smiling when I left her."

"That's Billie," she said.

"Who is she?" Clint asked. "Your daughter?"

"No, my niece," Mrs. Evans said. "Her mother was my younger sister. She died when Billie was five—that was almost twelve years ago. Billie's a lot like her mother—head strong."

"I see."

"Come with me," she said. "I'll show you to your room, and then you can see to your horse."

"Thank you."

She took him to a good sized room on the second floor with a comfortable bed, a chest of drawers and a wooden chair. Then she told him the schedule for breakfast and supper, and that he'd be on his own for lunch.

She took him back to the front door and told him what time the door would lock.

"I'll remember," he said. "I might as well take care of my horse, now. I passed a livery across from the police station."

"There's one closer. Just keep going to the end of Clarke Street and you'll see it. It's smaller, and less expensive."

"Thank you," he said. "I'll find it."

"I'll see you later, then, for supper."

"I'm, uh, sorry about Billie—" he started, but Mrs. Evens stopped him.

"Don't apologize," she said. "I'm afraid my niece makes her own decisions, and has for some time."

"Is she prepared for the consequences?" he asked.

"Apparently, she is," the woman said, "because she's been doing it since she was twelve."

"Well," Clint said, "she's apparently an even more interesting girl than I originally thought she was."

"Just don't tell her that you think she's interesting," Mrs. Evans said. "Please."

Chapter Four

Clint found the livery Mrs. Evans had told him about and made arrangements for Eclipse's care. After that he returned to the rooming house to leave his rifle, bedroll and saddlebags in his room. He made it in and out of the house without running into Mrs. Evens or other tenants.

He took a long walk around town, then, found that the good will and manners he'd run into earlier continued no matter where he went. It made him wonder about the three men he'd seen chasing Billie on the beach. What had gotten them so riled up that they'd chase a teenage girl?

He decided to take his questions to the place where most questions got answered in any town.

***

The Beach Grove Saloon was busier than it had been when he was there earlier, but for a saloon doing a brisk business, it was remarkably quiet. He looked around as he entered, did not see any girls working the floor. Also, there was no indication of any gambling being available, not even a pick-up poker game.

He approached the bar and it took the bartender a moment to notice him.

"Ah, you're back," he said. "Did you settle into one of the hotels?"

"Actually, I found a rooming house I liked. It was recommended to me."

"Well, as long as you're staying."

"For a while. How about a beer?"

"Coming up."

When he brought it Clint asked, "What's your name?"

"Oh, sure," the bartender said, "we haven't been introduced. I'm Jerry." He extended his hand.

Clint shook it and said, "I'm Clint."

"Nice to meet you. Excuse me."

Jerry went to serve some other customers, leaving Clint to look around again. All he saw were pleasant faces and smiles. He didn't see a lot of that in the saloons he was used to. Maybe later, when some of these men were drunk, it would change.

"I'm back," Jerry said.

"Everybody looks so happy," Clint said.

"And why not?" he asked. "They're getting everything they want here."

"What about girls? Gambling?"

"There are other places for that."

"I wasn't just talking about here, though," Clint said. "I was talking about the whole town. Why does everybody seem so happy?"

"Is that unusual?"

"It is where I'm from."

"Then maybe it's because these people aren't from where you're from."

"I guess so."

"Have you been around town?"

"I took a long walk before I came here," Clint said.

"Well, we've got some good restaurants, and if you are looking for girls and gambling—"

"Right now, I think I better get back to my rooming house for supper," Clint said. "I don't want to insult my landlady on my first night there."

"Which one is it?" Jerry asked

"I don't know if it has a name," Clint said. "It's on Clarke Street."

"Clarke Street?" Jerry seemed surprised.

"That's right. Do you know it?"

"I've heard of it," Jerry said. "The landlady's name is Evans, right?"

"That's right," Clint said. "Can you tell me—"

"Sorry," Jerry said, "but I've got work to do."

Clint felt a definite damper in Jerry's usually ebullient personality at the mention of Mrs. Evans' rooming house.

Chapter Five

When Clint got back to the rooming house he found the table in the dining room set up for supper, but he was puzzled by the fact that there were only three places set.

"Am I late?" he asked, when Mrs. Evans came out of the kitchen carrying a basket of biscuits.

"No," she said, "you're right on time, in fact."

"But . . . I only see three places," Clint said. "Are there only two other guests?"

"No," she said. "One of these places is for me."

"Ah," he said, "so one more guest."

"No," she said, "in fact, you're the only guest we have, right now."

"But there's another—"

"Have a seat, Mr. Adams," she said. "I'll bring supper right out."

"Yes, all right," he said. "Thank you. I'll just go to my room to wash up."

"All right. When you come back, sit anywhere," she said, and returned to the kitchen.

He went up to his room, used the pitcher-and-basin to wash his hands and face, then decided to change his shirt before he went back down.

When he returned to the dining room the table was covered with food—chicken, beef, vegetables, biscuits, pitchers of what looked like lemonade.

He chose a seat and sat down. Mrs. Evans appeared from the kitchen and said, "You may start eating."

"I was waiting for you."

"How polite," she said, taking a seat.

"Shall we wait for the third person?"

"She's in the kitchen," Mrs. Evans said. "She'll be here any minute. Go ahead and start."

He helped himself to a piece of chicken, and a slice of beef, then surrounded them with vegetables. He cut a piece of beef and put it in his mouth, where it almost melted. He was about to compliment her when the kitchen door opened and the third diner entered.

"It smells great Aunt Janet," Billie said. "I'm staved—" She stopped short when she saw Clint. "You made it!" she said.

"So did you."

She sat down at the table and smiled at him. Her face was clean and she was very pretty.

"My aunt's a great cook," she said, filling her plate.

"I can tell," Clint said. This time he had some chicken. Same result. It was delicious. "Everything tastes wonderful," he told Janet Evans.

"Thank you."

"When did you get back?" he asked Billie.

"It took me a little longer to get here than it took you," she said, "but I wasn't far behind you. There are shortcuts you can take on foot."

"Do you want to tell me now why those men were chasing you?"

She stuffed a biscuit into her mouth and then pointed, indicating that her mouth was too full to talk.

"Maybe after supper, then," he said.

She shrugged and kept eating.

He turned his attention to Janet Evans.

"Why don't you have any other boarders?" he asked.

"That's something I'd like to know," she replied.

"Well," he said, "if you get the word out about this food, I think that might do the trick."

"I'll work on that," she said.

It seemed that neither of the ladies was willing to talk while they ate, so the rest of the meal went by in silence.

"If you'd like," Janet Evans said after supper, "I can bring some coffee out to the front porch for you."

"I'd like that a lot," Clint said. "Thanks."

"You can smoke out there, if you like."

"I don't really smoke."

As she and Billie cleared the table, Clint went out to the front porch. The house was at the end of the street, and he could see lights lit on both sides of the street ahead of him. He paused and listened, but there was nothing to listen to. No voices, no music, no noise of any kind.

There were several chairs on the porch so he chose one and sat down. The front door opened, and Billie came out, carrying a cup of coffee.

"Here ya go," she said, handing it to him.

"Thank you," he said. "I have to say, you look much better wearing a dress and with a clean face."

"Thank you," she said, lifting her chin. "I'm a pretty girl."

"Yes, you are."

"Would you like to be my boyfriend?"

"No."

"Why not?"

"I'm too old for you," he said. "Besides, you wouldn't want me to be your boyfriend."

"Why not?"

"Well, as I said," he answered, "I'm too old for you. Or—let me put this another way—you're too young for me."

"How about Aunt Janet?"

"What about her?"

She pulled a chair over and sat next to him.

"Would you like to be her boyfriend?" she asked. "I mean, she ain't too young for you, is she?"

"Well, no, but——" "

"And she sure can cook."

"Yes, she can, but—"

"Then what's the problem?" Billie asked. "Oh, wait." She covered her mouth with her hands. "Is she too old?"

"No, no, that's not it, either."

"Then what—"

"If you'd shut up for a minute I'll tell you," he said cutting her off.

She recoiled, stung for a moment, but then her shoulders relaxed and she said, "Okay, so tell me."

"I'm not looking for a wife," he said. "Not now, and not ever."

"I didn't say nothin' about a wife," Billie replied. "I said girlfriend."

"I'm not looking for a girlfriend right now, either, Billie," he said. "I'm sorry."

"Okay, okay," she said, "so you don't have to be boyfriend and girlfriend. But you could just . . . you know. Be together . . . that way."

"What are you, some kind of a matchmaker?"

"I just think my aunt's . . . mood would change if she was with a man."

"I see," Clint said, "you're not trying to help me or her, you're trying to help yourself."

"It would help all of us, I think," Billie said.

"Well," Clint said, "you'll just have to find another way to change your aunt's mood. Maybe if you behaved better?"

Abruptly, Billie stood up.

"I'm going to bed," she said.

"Good idea."

She started for the door, then turned to look at him over her shoulder. There was a decidedly kittenish look on her face that surprised Clint and changed his entire opinion about her.

"If you come creepin' into my room tonight," she said, "I'll scream—maybe."

Chapter Six

Clint spent a quiet and restful night in his room at Janet Evans' rooming house. The bed was very comfortable. When he came downstairs the table was set for breakfast. There were eggs, ham steaks, potatoes, and biscuits, as well as the strong smell of coffee.

"Smells wonderful," he said to Janet.

"Do you have to wear your gun to the table?" she asked.

"I have to wear my gun all the time."

"All right, then. Sit and begin eating," she said. "I'll be out in a few minutes."

"And Billie?" Clint asked. "Will she be joining us?"

She stopped at the kitchen door. "I'm afraid my niece is already out looking for new trouble."

Clint had filled his plate with food by the time Janet reappeared. She sat at the opposite end of the table from him, which was pretty far away considering you could have fit four more on either side of them.

"So tell me," Clint said, "what kind of trouble does Billie usually find?"

"The teenage kind," Janet said.

"Do you mean, fighting, stealing . . . boys?" Clint asked.

"All of it, I'm afraid," she said. "I suppose you deserve to know, since you helped her. It's not always just boys."

"Men?" Clint asked. "How old is she?"

"She's seventeen, but you've seen her," Janet said. "She's pretty."

"That's true, but—"

"Don't tell me she didn't try to turn her feminine wiles on you," Janet said.

"Not really," Clint said.

"No?"

"Well," Clint said, "just for a moment, last night, when she was going to bed."

"Ah-ha. And how did you respond?"

"Like a grown man dealing with a child," Clint said, "which is what I was."

"What else did you talk about out there last night?" she asked.

"Well, we talked about you."

"Me?"

"She brought you up."

"What was she—what did she say?"

"She was talking about your . . . moods."

"My moods?'

"She seemed to think your moods need some . . . adjustment." He was trying not to insult her.

"In what way?"

"She seemed to think—you know, this ham is really good. What did you—"

"Mr. Adams," she said, "I don't think we were talking about ham, were we?"

"Maybe you should talk to your niece about this," he suggested.

"I think I'd prefer to hear it from you."

"Well, she seemed to think that you need a . . . man."

"I need a man? For what?"

"To improve your mood by—well, you know—um, having sex."

"Did she say that?"

"She didn't say 'sex,' but I got the point she was trying to make."

"And did she have a particular man in mind?" she asked.

"Well . . . do you think it might have been one of the men who were chasing her yesterday?"

"I don't know," she said. "She didn't tell me who was chasing her. Did she mention any men in particular?"

"Well . . . she asked me if I wanted to be your, uh, boyfriend."

She hesitated a moment, then said, "Sometimes she's such a child."

"First she asked if I wanted to be her boyfriend."

"And what did you say to that?"

"That I was too old. That's when she asked about you."

"And what was your response to that?"

"I told her the truth," he said.

"Which is?"

"I'm not looking for a girlfriend."

"I see."

"I mean, I'm just traveling to relax," he said. "I thought I'd come and see the ocean. And then somebody told me about lighthouses."

"Point Pinos."

"Yes," Clint said, "that one was mentioned. Where is it?"

"It's the closest to us," she said. "It illuminates Monterey Bay at night."

"How does it work?"

"That I don't know."

"Is there anyone living there?"

"There's a keeper," she said. "At the moment it's a woman named Emily Fish."

"Really? A woman? What's she like?"

"She has a reputation," Janet said. "Would you like some more coffee?"

"Yes, thank you."

She stood up, picked up the pot, walked to his end of the table to refill his cup, then returned to her own seat.

"So?" he asked. "What's she like?"

"She has a . . . reputation."

"As what?"

"She throws parties," Janet said. "A lot of them. In fact, the newspapers have called her 'the Socialite Keeper.' "

"Is that a fact? Have you been to many of her parties?" he asked.

"I haven't been to a single one."

"Not invited?"

"Actually," she said, "she invites most of the business owners in town. I just haven't . . . had the time to attend."

"Hmm," Clint said. "I wonder if she'd let me go out and have a look."

"I'm sure she would," Janet said. "She's very proud of that lighthouse."

"Emily Fish, you said?"

"Yes."

"I think I'll take a ride out, then, and see if Miss Fish will give me a tour."

"Mrs."

"What?"

"I believe," Janet said, "she is Mrs. Fish."

"She's married?"

"A widow," Janet said. "I understand she lives there alone."

Clint took another slice of ham and said, "This could be interesting."

Chapter Seven

After breakfast Clint offered to help Janet clean up.

"Don't be silly," she said. "That's what you're paying me for. You have things you want to do today."

"Yes, I do," he said, rising from his chair. "If I see Billie, do you want me to tell her anything?"

"Nobody can tell that girl anything," Janet said. "She has a mind of her own."

She turned and went into the kitchen.

Clint went out the front door and walked up Clarke Street, toward the center of town. He wanted to see if he could learn a little more about Emily Fish before he rode out to the lighthouse.

***

The local newspaper was called *The Pacific Courier*. He found the office and entered, asked the editor if he could see some past issues.

"I'd like to use them to learn something about your town," he said.

"Well, of course," the editor said. "Have a seat and I'll bring you some."

Clint sat at a table for a couple of hours, going through past issues of the *Courier*. There were many articles about new businesses opening, quite a few about the lighthouse and its keeper, Mrs. Fish.

"Are you finished already?" the editor asked, when Clint reappeared in his office.

"Yes," Clint said. "Can I help you put them away?"

The man, tall and rail thin, weaved an ink stained hand and said, "I have someone who can do that. What's your interest, friend?"

"The lighthouse," Clint said, "and its keeper."

"Ah," the man said, "the lovely Mrs. Fish."

"Lovely? Is she?"

"Oh yes." The man extended his hand. "Excuse me, I never introduced myself. Charles Ferguson, Publisher and Editor of the paper."

Clint shook his hand and said, "Clint Adams."

"Adams?" Ferguson dropped his hand and took a step back. "The Gunsmith?"

"That's right."

"Are you here—are you looking for someone?"

"No," Clint said, "I'm just looking for a little peace and quiet. And then I heard about the lighthouse. I thought I'd like to see it, but I wanted to do some re-search first."

"Well," Ferguson said, "you can ride out there. I'm sure the lady will show you around."

"So I've been told."

"She likes men," Ferguson went on, "especially famous ones. She'll probably throw a party in your honor."

"Oh, no," Clint said, "no party. I don't want a party. Like I said, I just want some peace and quiet."

"You'll have to tell her that, then," Ferguson said. "How long were you planning on staying in town?"

"I'm not sure," Clint said. "A few days."

"And then?"

"I'll probably go to Monterey."

"What are the chances I could get an interview before you leave?" the newspaperman asked.

"Not good," Clint said. "I'm afraid I don't give interviews."

"Ah," Ferguson said. "Well, maybe you'll change your mind. I'll be here if you do."

"Thanks for the newspapers," Clint said.

"Sure."

He left the office, feeling kind of bad for refusing the interview. The man had, after all, let him peruse old newspapers for two hours. Maybe he would change his mind . . . later.

Chapter Eight

Clint decided to just ride out to the lighthouse and see what he could see. He collected Eclipse at the livery and asked the hostler for directions.

"Everybody knows where that is," the old man said. "You just gotta ride out to the water."

"I've been to the water," Clint said, "and I didn't see the lighthouse, so I need something a little more specific."

The old man shrugged and gave him very detailed directions.

***

Point Pinos was located about halfway between Pacific Grove and Monterey. Clint was able to see it well before he reached it.

Actually, he was able to see the uppermost tip of the lighthouse, but when he reached it he was surprised. The lighthouse seemed to be stuck on top of a two story wood-frame house.

He reined Eclipse in and dismounted, stepped up onto the porch and approached the front door.

There was no response to his first knock, so he knocked again. When the door was opened by a woman he was surprised. The editor has said she was lovely, but he had understated the facts.

She was tall, willowy and blonde, with the kind of face that would stop men dead in their tracks. Even though she gave him only a bemused half smile and not a full one, it transformed the day.

"Hello," she said, "can I help you?"

"Uh, yes," he said, "I was told about this lighthouse over in Pacific Grove, where I'm staying. They said that you give tours."

"Well," she said, "not official tours—I was just upstairs cleaning the lens, which is why I didn't respond the first time you knocked." She was wearing a pair of jeans and what looked like a man's shirt, only she didn't fill it out the way a man would have.

"I'm sorry," he said, "I didn't mean to interrupt you. I just thought I'd ride out and see—"

"Well," she said, cutting him off, "since you rode all the way out here, I'm not about to send you away. Come inside."

"Thank you."

"Is your horse all right?" she asked. "He's not tied . . ."

"He won't go anywhere," he assured her.

"I hope not," she said. "What a beautiful animal."

He found himself in a front hall as she closed the door behind them.

"This way, please," she said, and led him into a smartly appointed parlor. It looked very neat to him, but she said, "Excuse the mess. Today is my day to work on the lens, and the upstairs."

"No problem."

"In fact," she said, "since I'm sure that's exactly what you're here to see, why don't we go upstairs?"

"I'd like to introduce myself first," Clint said. "My name is Clint Adams."

"Mr. Adams," she said, extending her hand, "my name is Emily Fish. I'm very pleased to meet you." He thought she held his hand a little longer than was necessary, giving him time to study her face. She was definitely more woman than girl, probably in her mid-thirties and the only word that could rightly describe her was beautiful.

"Shall we go?" she asked.

"Please," he said, "lead the way."

He followed her to a stairway and afforded her the respect of not staring at her behind as they went up. He took a quick, admiring look, but that was it.

"This is the Navigation Room," she said, as they reached the top.

He looked around. There were a couple of desks with charts on them, some navigational tools, and also a chart hanging on the wall.

"And the lens is in here." She went through another doorway, and he followed. "We have to go up again," she said.

He was impressed. There was a large light in the center of the room, with more than one lens, designed to magnify the light from inside. All around them was glass, just glass.

"If you look out there," she said, "you'll see all of Monterey Bay."

Together, they stood at the glass and stared out. There was a catwalk that ran all the way around the lens house.

"Without this light, ships would come into this bay and find themselves floundering on the rocks."

"This is very impressive." He was looking at her profile when he spoke. She was still staring out at the water.

"Would you like facts about the lens?"

"Sure."

She turned to look at the lens, and he turned with her.

"This lens is a Fresnel Lens, created by a Frenchman, Augustine Fresnel. The flame inside burns with whale oil, and the lens focuses it into a strong narrow beam that shines out to sea." She looked at him. "It's my job to keep the lens burning, and to keep it clean."

"It looks like you know your job," he said.

"That is because I've been cleaning it all morning. But if you were here at night, you would be able to see how strong the beam is, and how far out it shines."

Clint didn't know for sure, but that sounded like an invitation.

"Would you like to go out on the catwalk?" she asked.

"That'd be great."

She opened a door and stepped out, and he followed. The catwalk was constructed of metal and felt odd beneath his feet. He looked down at the ground below.

"How far up are we?" he asked.

"It's eighty-nine feet," she said.

He stared out at the sea again, felt the salt air on his face.

"This is a beautiful place to live, let alone work," he said to her.

"Yes, it is," she said. Her hair was tied behind her head, but a wisp or two had come loose and were blowing in the wind.

"Why don't we go back downstairs?" she said. "I have some lemonade."

"That sounds good."

Again, she led the way, taking him all the way back down to the main floor.

Chapter Nine

She took him to the kitchen, where he sat at a well-made wooden table while she retrieved a pitcher of iced lemonade and poured two glasses. Once that was done, she sat across from him. Again she apologized for "the mess," when all he saw was a neat and clean room.

"Do you have any more questions?" she asked.

"Yes," he said, "do you ever get out of here?"

"I meant about the lighthouse."

"Oh," he said, "no, you've been very informative. I couldn't have asked for more. I appreciate it. I was just wondering if you ever go into town—you know, for a meal, for instance?"

"Not really," she said. "On occasion, however, I've been known to invite people out here. If you've done your research, you've read about me. I believe they call me the 'Socialite Keeper'?"

"What makes you think I researched you?"

"I doubt that the Gunsmith goes anywhere without knowing what he's walking into. Oh yes," she said, as he looked surprised, "I recognized your name. To a much greater extent, you know what it's like to have the newspapers brand you with a name."

"I think it's different in my case," Clint said. "Do you mind it so much?"

"As nicknames go," she said, "I suppose it's not so bad. What about you?"

"As nicknames go," he said, "I've had that one too long to be able to do anything about it now, don't you think?"

"I suppose you're right."

He finished his lemonade and said, "I should let you get back to work."

They both stood up, and she walked him to the door.

"I have an idea," she said. "Come back tonight, after dark. I'll let you see the light while it's in operation."

"That sounds like a good idea," he said. "Thank you for the invitation."

She opened the door and he stepped out onto the porch.

"This will give me time to clean the place up," she said.

"When I come back," he said, "can I call you Emily?"

She smiled and said, "Only if I can call you Clint."

This time her smile was full, and he doubted the light in the lighthouse could match its brilliance.

"It's a deal," he said.

Chapter Ten

He rode back to town and stopped at the livery.

"You get to see the lighthouse?" the hostler asked.

"I did."

"And the lighthouse lady?"

"I saw her, too. I'm going to be needing my horse again later this evening," Clint told the man. "Around dusk."

"I'll have him ready," the man promised.

Clint nodded and left the livery, walked back toward the rooming house. When he reached it, though, he decided to keep going and stop in the first saloon he saw for a cold beer.

***

He found a small one called The Shamrock for some reason and went inside. There were a few patrons seated at tables, and nobody at the small bar.

The bartender looked like an ex-boxer, with thick arms and shoulders, a flattened nose, and thinning grey/black hair.

"Getcha somethin'?"

"Cold beer."

"Comin' up."

He set the beer down in front of Clint and moved away, even though there was nobody else demanding his attention. A bartender who didn't want to talk. What was Clint going to find next in this odd town?

He drank the beer, purging his taste buds of the lemonade Emily Fish had given him. Under normal circumstances, in a Western town, he would have looked for a poker game to while away the hours until he was to return to the lighthouse again. But according to Jim, the bartender in the Beach Grove Saloon, those were hard to find. Unless you knew where to look.

Maybe all bartenders knew.

"Excuse me," Clint said.

The bartender heard him and came over.

"Another one?"

"No, thanks, that one was good," Clint said. "Do you have any idea where a man might find a poker game in this town?"

"Not here, I can tell you that," the man said. "I think you'd have to try one of the larger saloons in town."

"You don't know of any . . . private games?"

"Sorry," the man said. "I ain't sayin' you'll find a game in one of the bigger saloons, but one of those bartenders might be able to help you."

"Okay," Clint said. "Thanks."

"Come back if you want another beer," the man said. "That much I can help you with."

"I'll remember."

Clint turned and left.

***

Instead of going into one of the other large saloons, he decided to go back to the Beach Grove Saloon.

"Ah, my friend returns," Jim said, spreading his arms. "What'll be?"

It was roughly the same time it had been the day before when he first entered the saloon. As he looked around he swore he saw the same faces on the half dozen men who were there.

"A beer," Clint said.

"What have you been up to this morning?" Jim asked, as he served the beer.

"I went out to see the lighthouse."

"Ah," Jim said, "and what did you think?"

"It's impressive."

"And the lady Keeper?"

"Also impressive. I'm going back out again tonight, to see it in action."

"The light?"

"Yes, of course the light," Clint said.

Jim shrugged. "I was just askin'."

Clint sipped from his glass.

"What do you plan to do now?"

"I was thinking about what you said yesterday."

"About girls?" Jim leaned in. "I can tell you where there's a fine cat house—"

"Not girls," Clint said. "I was talking about poker."

"Ah," Jim said, "you want to gamble."

"I want to relax," Clint said, "and kill some time."

"Well," Jim said, rubbing his jaw, "I can tell you where there's a dice game."

"I'm not interested in dice," Clint said. "I prefer cards."

"Ah ha," Jim said, "well, I do know where you can find a Faro table—"

"Not Faro," Clint said.

"Blackjack?"

Clint shook his head.

"So only poker?" Jim asked.

"Yes," Clint said, "just poker."

"High stakes?"

"Not necessarily," Clint said. "Just enough to make the passing of time interesting."

"There might be a game," Jim said. "I'll have to find out, though."

"How long?"

"Should take about an hour."

"I'll come back."

Chapter Eleven

If there had been a sheriff in Pacific Grove, Clint would have gone to see him, just to check in and let the man know he was there. He did that in most western towns he visited, just to avoid trouble. But somehow he didn't feel the same obligation to the Pacific Grove Police Department. He did, however, walk past the police department building again, saw two uniformed policemen come walking out, exchanged a nod with them.

He stopped into a small café and had a cup of coffee, then made his way back to the saloon.

"Found you a game," Jim said when Clint walked to the bar. "Let me get one of these guys to cover the bar for me and I'll walk you over there."

Jim went over to a table and tapped a man on the shoulder, spoke to him briefly. The man nodded, stood up and moved in behind the bar.

"Okay, let's go," Jim said.

Out on the street Clint said, "Where are we going?"

"A hotel, a small one," Jim said, "but the rooms are pretty good."

"That's where the game is?"

"Yup."

"Is it a regular game?"

"Pretty regular, but they've agreed to let you play."

"Because . . ."

"Well . . . because I told them who you are."

"Great," Clint said. "Are they going to want to play poker with me, or shoot me?"

"They play poker," Jim said. "All the players are business owners from town. That means no hotheads with guns."

"That part sounds good."

"Also," Jim said, "you should be aware that one of the players is the Chief of Police."

"Interesting to know."

"That's it, just up ahead," Jim said.

"The Hotel Seascape?"

"That's it."

"Do all the hotels and saloons around here have the ocean in the name?"

"It doesn't take much imagination, does it?" the bartender admitted.

They entered the small hotel and went right by the front desk, with Jim giving the clerk a friendly nod.

Clint followed Jim to the second floor, and down a short hall. At the end of the hall was a closed door that the bartender knocked on. It was opened an inch so an eye could examine the two of them, and then it was opened wide.

"Hello, Jim," a man said. "Come on in."

Clint followed Jim into the room. In the center was a round table with four individuals sitting at it. The fifth had answered the door. Now he retook his seat. Clint decided to wait for an introduction. But he was already surprised by the identity of one of the players.

"This is Clint Adams," Jim said. "He's interested in playing some poker."

"So you told us," one man said. He was large, with a barrel chest, deep voice, and impressive head of steel grey hair. "Mr. Adams, have a seat and we'll make introductions."

"Thanks," Clint said.

"My name is Albert Anderson," the big man said. "I'm the Chief of Police in Pacific Grove."

"Nice to meet you."

"The man who let you in is Mike Whaley, he owns two cafés in town. Then there's Lou Hackett, who owns the local theater, and Andy Barrett."

"I'm a lawyer," Barrett said.

"And the lady," the Chief said, "is Mrs. Janet Evans. She owns—"

"The lady and I are acquainted," Clint said.

"Why don't we explain to Mr. Adams what our stakes are?" Janet suggested.

Chapter Twelve

The game was not high stakes, but neither was it penny ante. In a matter of hours a man—or woman—could lose a decent amount of money. Given enough time, a player's property could become endangered. Of course, someone would have to play long and lose that much to reach that point.

Clint was surprised that the best players at the table seemed to be the Chief of Police, and Janet Evans. The other men pushed their luck too much, tried to fill hands where the odds were not good. After a couple of hours he was well ahead.

Jim the bartender had left soon after Clint sat down. Unlike other games Clint had played in, there was very little conversation included. He was surprised that after about two-and-a-half hours the Chief of Police, Anderson, started to talk.

"So tell me, Mr. Adams," Anderson said, "aside from taking my money, what brought you to Pacific Grove? From what I've heard of you, this is not your usual bailiwick."

"That's exactly the reason I came here," Clint said. "I was looking to spend some time away from my usual haunts. I thought coming to the ocean would be interesting. And then I heard about the lighthouse."

"Ah yes," Anderson said, "Point Pinos. You definitely should go out and see that."

"I have," Clint said, "I was there late this morning, and I'm going back to tonight."

"Tonight?"

"To see the light in action."

"Ah," Anderson said. "Did Mrs. Fish invite you?"

"She did."

"Interesting," the lawyer, Barrett said. "I don't recall her ever giving private tours. Usually, she just has one of her parties."

"Maybe," Janet Evans said, "Mr. Adams made a favorable impression on her."

"Indeed," Anderson said, "perhaps he did."

"In fact," Clint said, looking at the clock on the wall, "I'll have to get going in a couple of hours."

"Good," Barrett said, "that gives us some time to try to get our money back."

"So deal, Barrett," Anderson said, "and let's get to it."

***

Several hours later Clint was still ahead. He noticed that Janet was even further in the black than he was. The chief was winning, but the others were all still trying to get their money back and succeeding only in losing even more.

"Time for me to pack it in," Clint said.

"That's not right," Barrett said, "leaving while you're ahead."

"I know," Clint said, "you'd prefer I leave while behind, but that really isn't the point, is it?"

"He's right," Janet said. "It's time for me to go, too." She looked at Clint with no real expression on her face. "Would you walk me back to the house?"

"Of course."

They both collected their winnings from the table and started for the door.

"Don't worry boys," the chief said, as they went out the door, "I'm still here. Deal the cards."

***

Clint walked Janet back to the rooming house. It was not dark yet, but dusk was coming.

"Are you coming inside?" she asked.

"Only to clean up," he said. "Then I have to ride to the lighthouse."

"To see Mrs. Fish?"

"To see the lens."

"I see. Well, I'm going to have a cup of coffee. Do you want one before you go?"

"Sure, thanks," Clint said. "I'll have it when I come down."

They went inside and split up. Janet went to the kitchen, and Clint went to his room.

When he came down he smelled coffee, but didn't see any in the parlor or the dining room.

"Janet," he called.

"Have a seat," she called from the kitchen. "I'll be right out with the coffee."

He sat down on the sofa to wait. Through a window he saw that it was now dusk. He only needed to get there after dark, which gave him plenty of leeway to have a cup of coffee with his beautiful landlady.

"Well, here it is," she said.

He turned his head and saw her standing in front of the kitchen door, holding two cups of coffee. She had taken the opportunity to change out of the dress she'd been wearing to the poker game.

Now all she was wearing was a smile.

Chapter Thirteen

She walked into the parlor, had to lean over to set the cups down on the table in front of the sofa. Her pale, smooth breasts swayed, larger than they had seemed when she was dressed. Her nipples were dark brown.

"You're a beautiful woman, Janet," Clint said, "but what's this about?"

"Don't tell me you haven't wondered how we'd be," she said, standing up straight. "I have, ever since you walked through the door."

"What about Billie—"

"She won't be back for hours," Janet said. "If she comes back at all before morning."

"I have an appointment—"

"I know," she said, "with that hussy out at the lighthouse."

"Is that why you're doing this?"

"Yes," she said. "To get to you before she does."

"But I'm only going out there to see the lens while it's lit."

"And she invited you, right?"

"That's right."

She put her hand out to him. "Come on. I'm going to give you something to think about while you're with her."

He looked at her hand, then her naked breasts, her beautiful face, and finally breathed in the scent that was wafting up from between her thighs.

He took her hand.

He was only human, after all.

Clint was in a sort of a daze as she led him into her bedroom. Janet Evans just didn't seem to be this kind of woman. There had been nothing in her demeanor to make him think they'd end up here.

She turned to him and he could feel the heat off her body.

"What about that gun?" she asked.

"Here," he said, unbuckling the gunbelt and removing it. He walked to the bed and hung it on the bedpost.

"While you're there," she said, "you might as well take the rest off."

He took off his clothes while she watched, her arms folded and one eyebrow cocked. It was a pose he found oddly sensual.

When he was naked his cock was fully hard. She unfolded her arms and stared at him, a hungry look suddenly in her eyes—and just like that she was a totally different woman.

She approached him, took him into her hands while staring into his eyes. He leaned forward and kissed her as her hands stroked him expertly. As a widow, she'd certainly had experience with sex, and it showed. Her husband had been a lucky man.

As he kissed her he ran his hands down her back, stoked the globes of her ass, ran his finger along the crease between them, then turned her so that the backs of her legs were against the bed, and pushed her onto her back.

"Oh," she said, as he started to kiss her breasts, biting her nipples and running his hand up her thigh until his fingers poked into her pubic thatch. She was very wet and his fingers slid right in.

She gasped, reached down to grab his wrist and said, "Let's get on the bed the right way. I want you in me now!"

Clint decided since this was her idea, to give her exactly what she wanted.

They stood up, pulled the bedding down so she could lie on her back on the sheets. He mounted her and had no problem, his hard penis gliding right into her wet pussy. As he started to pound into her, the sheets beneath them grew wet from her juices. She gasped, wrapped her legs and arms around him, and held on for dear life. When she came she actually screamed. His own ending seemed anticlimactic . . .

Afterward she watched as he got dressed.

"I'm sorry," he said, "but I have to—"

"I understand," she said. "Go and see Mrs. Fish." She was lying on her back with her hands behind her head. "I like that you're going to see her while still smelling of me."

"I don't think it matters," he said. "After all I'm only—"

"—going to see the lens," she finished for him. "I know. You told me."

He grabbed his gunbelt from the bedpost and strapped it back on.

"There," she said, "you look very presentable."

He looked down at her, let his eyes roam over her naked body, and said, "So do you. I'm sorry I have to leave."

"I'll see you at breakfast in the morning," she said.

"I'll be back in a couple of hours—"

"I'm sure I'll be asleep," she said, "and Billie might be in the house."

"Right," he said. "Well, then . . . see you tomorrow."

"Don't worry, Clint," she said, grabbing the sheet and covering herself with it, "we'll have more time— that is, if you decide to stay longer."

"Right."

"Please make sure the front door locks when you leave," she called after him.

Chapter Fourteen

Janet's words played over and over in his head, about going to see Emily Fish while still smelling of her. Because of that, he made a hasty stop at a horse trough in town and did his best to wash some of his landlady's scent.

With that done he rode out to the lighthouse. It was dark, but eventually he was able to spot the light and head right for it.

When he got there he knocked on the door and Emily Fish answered.

"I thought you weren't coming," she said.

"It wasn't an easy ride in the dark," he told her, "but then I spotted your light."

She eyed him for a moment, and he wondered if she could tell what he'd been doing before coming there.

"Come in, then," she finally said.

He entered and turned to face her. The blonde woman was wearing a simple but colorful cotton dress, rather than the work clothes she'd had on earlier in the day. She also smelled as if she was fresh from a bath. Clint suddenly felt self-conscious about still smelling of Janet Evans' juices.

"Would you like a drink?" she asked. "I have some wine."

"That would be great."

"Come with me to the kitchen."

She led the way, and he watched while she poured two glasses of red wine.

"Why don't we take our glasses with us upstairs," she suggested, handing him one.

"That suits me," Clint said. "I can't wait to see that light up close."

She led the way up the stairs, talking as they went.

"You'll want to make sure you never look directly into the light," she said. "It would probably blind you, maybe permanently."

"I'll remember that," he said, "for sure."

When they reached the light they stood behind it, so Clint could look out at the bay, where the concentrated beam was pointing.

"Wow," he said, "look at that."

"Yes," she said, "it's very impressive."

"I've never seen a light that bright, or intense," he told her.

"There are many lighthouses along the California coast," she said, "but this one is the brightest."

"I can believe it," he said, "and I'll bet it's the cleanest."

"It's also the only one with a woman as the Keeper," she pointed out. "Shall we step outside?"

Out on that catwalk, he thought. In the dark?

"Naw," he said, "I think I'm good in here."

She turned and looked at him with an amused expression on her lovely face.

"Don't tell me the great Gunsmith is afraid of the dark," she said.

"No," he said, "it's not the dark. I'm just not crazy about being out there, eighty-nine feet up, combined with being in the dark."

"Well," she said, "I can't say I blame you for that. Why don't we go back downstairs? I have some cheese and crackers that would go wonderfully with this wine."

"Sounds good to me," he said. Playing poker hadn't left him much time for eating, and he found that he was very hungry.

He followed her back down to the kitchen, where she invited him to sit while she assembled the cheese and crackers and brought it to the table. She topped off their glasses and then sat opposite him.

"Well," she said, "this is nice."

"It's very nice," he said. "Thank you."

"You look hungry."

"I am," he said.

"No supper?"

"I got involved in a poker game."

"Did you win?"

"I did."

"But you didn't eat."

"I didn't."

He put some cheese on a cracker, stuck it in his mouth, chewed and washed it down with the wine.

"You know," she said, "I have some chicken leftover from my dinner."

"Oh, I don't want to put you out."

"It's no bother," she said. "Just talk to me while I get it and keep snacking on the cheese and crackers."

She got up to take the chicken from a storeroom behind the kitchen.

"The cool salt air helps me preserve my meat," she told him.

"There must be all kinds of advantages to living here," he said.

"It's always cool in the evenings," she said, "even in the summer." She turned to look at him. "Would you like the chicken heated?"

"Cold is fine," he said.

"Good," she said, "the sooner you're well fed the sooner we can get on to . . . other things."

Before he could ask her what she meant by that she turned back to her task.

Chapter Fifteen

The chicken had been baked with certain spices and was delicious. By the time Clint was finished, his hands and face were greasy.

Emily Fish sat across from Clint and watched him eat.

"It's been some time since I watched a man enjoy my food," she said.

"Your husband?"

She nodded.

"What about when you have your parties?"

"Then I have the food brought in from town," she said. "I do my cooking for myself."

"And now you're sharing it with me," Clint said. "Thank you."

"It's my pleasure," she said. "I've . . . enjoyed watching you eat."

She stood and cleaned the bones from in front of him, poured him another glass of wine. Bending to do so brought her very close to him—so close that the scent of her filled his nostrils—and, apparently, vice versa.

"Phew," she said, "you need a bath."

"I beg your pardon?" Could she smell Janet Evans on him?

"You're all greasy . . ." she said.

"I can wash in your sink—"

". . . and you smell as if you washed up in a horse trough."

"I . . . well . . ."

"I think I'll draw you a hot bath," she said. "You're not in a hurry to ride back to town tonight, are you?"

"Well, no—"

"Good," she said. "I have a wonderful bathtub—it's actually large enough for two."

"Um—"

"Come on," she said. "I'll show you where you can get undressed."

She left Clint in a small room where he undressed and then wrapped himself in a towel. She told him to just go through the other door when he was ready, and the bathtub would be there.

He had to admit he was curious. When he opened the door and saw the tub would she be in it? Or was he just reading something into her comments that wasn't there, because of what had happened with Janet Evans?

There was only one way to find out.

He stepped to the door with his gunbelt over his naked shoulder, opened it, walked through and saw—not without some disappointment—that the room was empty but for a wooden chair and a bathtub of steaming water.

Clint was in the tub, with his gunbelt hanging on the chair next to him. She had left him a fragrant bar of soap and a wash rag. He used both liberally, divesting himself of chicken grease, horse trough, and Janet Evans.

He was just rinsing soap out of his hair when the door opened, and Emily Fish stepped into the room.

Naked.

He stared at her, awed. She was the total opposite of Janet Evans' long and lean body. She had large breasts and wide hips, pink nipples and what seemed to be acres of flawless, pale skin. The bushy tangle of hair between her legs was even more golden than the hair on her head, if that was possible.

"Are you clean?" she asked.

"As I'll ever be," he managed to say.

"God," she said, approaching the tub, "then we can move on to what comes next."

"And what's that?" he asked.

She knelt down by the tub, looked down at his cock, which was now poking up from the water.

"I think you know," she said, reaching and taking hold of his cock.

"Emily—"

"Shhh," she said. "You'll scare him away." She began to stroke him, up and down.

"Oh," he said, reaching for her breasts, "I don't think he's going anywhere for a while."

***

Outside the lighthouse three men were standing and watching.

"When's he gonna leave?" Tom Prado asked.

"I don't know," Mitch Murrill said. "Stop askin' me."

Prado looked at the other man, Felix Archer, who just shrugged.

"That's the same sidewinder who snatched that gal from us on the beach," Prado said.

"I know that!" Murrill said.

"Who the hell is he?"

Murrill looked at Prado, then Archer.

"Yeah, okay," he said. "Let's go to town and find out."

Chapter Sixteen

He tried to draw her into the tub with him—it was, as she'd said, big enough for two people—but she continued to tease him from the outside, letting him touch her while she ran her hands over his chest and thighs, stroked his penis and caressed his balls. But she wouldn't let him pull her into the water.

"So this was your plan when you invited me this morning?" he asked.

"Oh, I thought something might happen," she said. "It's been a while for me, and you're more man than I've seen in quite some time—maybe since my husband died." She tightened her hand on his hard cock. "In fact, in some ways you remind me of him."

"You mean . . ." he looked down at her hand.

"Yes," she said, "the way you eat."

Abruptly, she released him and stood up, taking her wondrous breasts out of his reach. He found himself staring at her pubic bush.

"What now?" he asked. "You want to tease me some more?"

"Hardly," she said. "I think it's time for me to join you in the tub."

"Finally!" he said.

***

Billie watched from behind a tree as the three men crept away from the lighthouse to where they had hidden their horses. She watched them ride away, presumably toward town.

She turned and walked back to the lighthouse. Clint Adams' horse was still outside. Billie smiled. She knew that Clint had been in the house with her aunt for some time, tonight. Now he was in the lighthouse with Emily Fish.

She thought it was all very funny.

***

Emily Fish stepped gracefully into the tub and sat opposite Clint. Idly, she soaped her big breasts while he watched. As she rinsed them he saw how distended the pink nipples had become.

Her legs were inside his, her bare feet rubbing his inner thighs, and brushing his cock and balls. He reached down to rub her feet, and calves.

"I'm impressed," she said.

"Why?"

"You're patient."

He wondered if he would have been as patient if he hadn't just had sex with Janet Evans a matter of hours ago.

"You don't seem to be in a hurry," he said.

"I'm not," she said. "I intend to enjoy every second of this, and I'll make it worth your while if you don't turn into a brute on me."

"Well," he said, "later, maybe."

***

Billie let herself into the lighthouse quietly. She stopped just inside to listen. When she didn't hear anything, she moved further inside. When she realized they were nowhere in the parlor or kitchen, she wondered if they had gone up to the light. But then she heard something that changed her mind. She crept to the door outside the room where Emily kept her large bathtub and pressed her ear to it. She heard talking, but nothing else. If they were in the bathtub together, they weren't doing anything yet but bathing. But that would change.

She smiled. What would they do if she stripped naked and walked in to join them? If Clint Adams had been alone, or with some woman other than Emily, she might have done it, just to see his reaction. But she wasn't willing to do that to Emily. She knew how long her friend had been without a husband. If she had gotten into the bathtub with Clint Adams, it was because he had something she wanted—or needed.

So, she'd leave them alone and let them do what they wanted to do. But that didn't mean she couldn't stay outside the door and listen.

But thinking about Clint Adams and Emily naked in the tub excited her. She unbuttoned her shirt, and undid her trousers . . .

***

Clint was trying to stay patient, but the more attention she paid to his cock the harder it became. However, he saw her nostrils flaring and chest heaving as her breathing became heavier, and in the end it was she who gave in first.

She pushed off from her end of the tub to join him on his, pressing herself against them. Their mouths fused together in their first kiss, and their eagerness was equal. Their hands roamed all over each other, and she positioned herself atop him so that his penis was trapped between them, her pubic area pressing his cock against his own belly. She began to run herself up and down against it, her breasts mashed against his chest.

When they broke their kiss he ran his lips over her neck, her shoulders, slipped his hands beneath her arms to lift her high enough so that he could kiss and suck her nipples. Having a woman's nipples in his mouth was one of his favorite things, and he suckled them hard until she not only moaned, but cried out.

***

Outside the room Billie was seated on the floor, her back to the door. Her shirt was completely unbuttoned, and with one hand she caressed her own breasts and nipples. Her other hand was inside her pants and underwear, touching herself where she was wet. She had been with boys and men, but they only poked her there, finished and then rolled off. She knew there were other things to be done, to make her feel good. It was good when she touched herself, so it probably would feel better if she could get a man to touch her there.

She wondered if Clint was touching Emily there? She could hear her moaning now, so they were doing something. She could even hear splashing.

She let out a little moan herself, but then stopped, afraid they'd hear her. Biting her lip she rubbed herself harder, and continued to listen . . .

***

Emily shifted herself so that she was no longer pinning Clint's erection between them. Now it was pointing stiffly toward the ceiling. She lifted her hips and sat on it, gasping as he slid into her wet depths.

"Oh God," she said, and started to ride him up and down, splashing water to the floor.

Neither of them heard it when Billie's back and head banged against the door as she experienced her own spasm.

Chapter Seventeen

Billie gasped and snatched her hand out of her pants. Aware that she had banged into the door with her head and back she hastily got to her feet and hurried down the hall on shaky legs.

In the parlor she stopped to button her shirt and do up her trousers. Then she sat down on the sofa and thought about what had just happened. Something had rushed through her body, something she had never felt before. She was shaking and her legs were weak. She needed a few minutes to calm down, and she hoped Emily and Clint Adams wouldn't be coming out any time soon.

At least, it didn't sound like they would.

***

Emily had her hands firmly planted on Clint's shoulders as she jumped up and down on his rigid cock. Her breasts bounced and jiggled in front of his face in a fascinating dance. Water continued to spill, and the tub even inched along the floor until finally she came down on him and stayed there, grinding their crotches together and biting her lip as she rode the waves of her orgasm. Her eyes fluttered and even, at one point, threatened to roll back in her head.

Clint lifted her gently and set her down on her side of the tub. The water had turned cool during their romp, so he got out and grabbed a towel.

"Come on," he said, holding it for her. "Time to get out before we shrivel up."

She smiled. "I don't know if my legs will stop shaking."

"I'm having the same problem."

As she stood and stepped from the tub he wrapped her in the towel.

"I think we should go to my bedroom," she said.

"Are you sleepy?"

"Hell, no," she said. "You don't think I'm done with you, do you?"

"Oh, you want more?"

She looked down at his semi-erect cock, then reached out and stroked it. Immediately, it began to harden again.

"Don't you?"

He grinned and said, "Let's go."

***

Billie heard the door open before she was ready to leave. Panicked, she jumped up from the sofa and hid behind it.

As Clint and Emily walked through the parlor together she sneaked a peek. Emily was wrapped in a towel, but Clint Adams was totally naked. Her eyes widened when she saw his penis. The boys, and few men, that she'd been with were no match for him. She grew excited again, but knew she had to stay hidden, and that she had to get out of there.

When they had passed through the parlor and gone up the stairs to Emily's bedroom, Billie rose from behind the sofa and hurriedly let herself out.

***

Murrill, Prado and Archer knew their way to town well, so getting there in the dark was no problem. When they arrived, they split up in order to try different saloons, to see if anyone knew who the stranger in town was. They agreed to meet at a saloon called The Whiskey Station.

Murrill got there first, got three glasses and a bottle of whiskey and settled down to wait. Before long Prado appeared, followed soon after by Archer. They all had the same information.

"Goddamnit," Prado said. "The Gunsmith."

"Why ain't he dead, yet?" Archer asked. "He's gotta be old."

"Well, he ain't dead," Murrill said, "and he's here."

"What are we gonna do?" Prado asked.

"Well, we ain't gonna let him change our plans," Murrill said. "I'll tell you that. That woman's got gold in that lighthouse, and we're gonna get it."

"Whataya think he was doin' there tonight?" Archer asked.

"What do you think?" Murrill said. "You've seen what the woman looks like."

"So he's gettin' his ashes hauled," Prado said. "Maybe he won't be back. Maybe he'll leave town."

"Well," Murrill said, "we won't know that for sure until mornin'."

"So we gotta wait?" Archer asked.

"We wait," Murrill said.

"I'm gettin' impatient," Prado said.

"Have a drink," Murrill said, pouring them each a shot. "Patience is gonna be worth it."

"It better be," Archer said.

They each downed their drink.

"Murrill," Archer said.

"Yeah?"

"You ain't thinkin' about tryin' to take the Gunsmith alone, are you?"

"I'm thinkin' about it," Murrill admitted, "but I probably won't try."

He poured three more drinks.

Chapter Eighteen

When they got to Emily's room Clint proceeded to dry her thoroughly with the towel, which only served to excite both of them, again. He tossed away the towel and looked her up and down. Her curves, her pale skin, her pink nipples, it was all as perfect as a woman could get.

"Finished looking?" she asked.

"Yes."

"Then start touching."

He reached out and took her breasts in his hands, cupping them, holding their smooth undersides as if weighing them. She closed her eyes as he used his thumbs to also stroke her nipples.

"You like nipples," she said.

"I love them," he said, "especially these."

She reached out to grasp his penis.

"Then perhaps we should get to bed, so you can pay them proper attention."

"That suits me."

He pulled her to him and kissed her, and locked together, they moved to the bed and fell onto it.

***

Billie let herself into the rooming house by the front door. Her Aunt Janet was in the parlor.

"Where have you been?" she asked.

"Out."

"Out where, young lady?"

"Just out."

"What have you been doing?" Janet asked. "Your clothes are disheveled."

"I was just . . . walking," Billie said. "I'm going to bed."

"Have you been with a boy?" Janet asked.

Billie turned.

"I haven't been with a boy in a long time, Aunt Janet," Billie said.

"Is that so?"

"I've outgrown boys."

Janet frowned.

"You mean . . ."

"Yes," Billie said, "I prefer men now, but to answer your question, no, I haven't been with anyone tonight."

Janet's shock showed on her face.

"Billie—"

"I'm going to bed, Aunt Janet," Billie said. "Good night."

Janet watched as her niece went up the stairs to her room. She sat down heavily on the sofa, her mind reeling. Was this her fault? If her mother—Janet's sister— had lived and raised her, would Billie have turned out this way?

That was something she'd never know.

***

"Ouch," Emily said.

"That hurt?" he asked.

"Well, of course," she said. "You're biting them."

"But you said—"

"I know what I said," she replied, interrupting him with a smile. "I'm not telling you to stop. I actually like the way it feels. Ouch! Ooh . . ."

He bit and sucked her nipples, slid his hand down over her belly, striking her thighs, her ass. He continued to caress her flanks as he suckled her, and could smell how wet she was growing.

"You know," she said, "you could pay attention to an entire other area."

"Oh," he said, moving his hand between her thighs, "you mean here?"

"Ooh . . . yes, I do mean there!"

Chapter Nineteen

Clint did not continue to minister to Emily's dripping pussy with his hand. Instead, he got down between her legs so he could taste her, delving into her with his tongue. She gasped and reached down to grab his head and hold it there as his tongue began to flutter.

"Oh, Jesus," she gasped. "Don't stop."

He had no intention of stopping until he knew she was done. He put his lips there to use as well as his tongue, while he kept his hands busy on her breasts.

She began to writhe beneath him, moving her legs, almost kicking if he hadn't had her pinned down with his elbows. As she got more and more wet, soaking his face as well as the sheets, he knew she was getting close. He managed to escape the grip of her hands and moved his face away from her.

"What are you doing?" she demanded. "Don't stop."

"I'm not stopping," he said, "just changing my position."

He mounted her, pressed the head of his cock against her, and then slid in easily. She gasped and wrapped her arms around him while spreading her legs wide. He pumped away at her and suddenly her body was overtaken by spasms that caused her to tense for a moment, the muscles of her body going taut, and then the next moment she was bucking beneath him. And then he exploded inside of her with a loud roar . . .

***

"My God," she said, sometime later. "I can't catch my breath."

"I know how you feel," he said, lying next to her.

"It's not just that it's been a long time for me," she said. "I've never been with a man like you. You seem to care about my pleasure as much as you do about yours—even more."

"I don't think this works unless we both enjoy it," he said.

"Well," she said, "I enjoyed it, and from the noise you made, so did you."

She sat up in bed and looked down at him.

"Are you hungry?"

"Yes," he said.

"Good. So am I. Let's go downstairs. I have more leftovers."

"I should get dressed."

"Why? Are you leaving?"

"I should go back to town—"

"I'm not through with you."

"Is that right?"

She smiled, put her hand on his thigh.

"I don't think you're finished with me, either."

"Well, no . . ." he said.

"And I mean tonight," she said. "We're not finished with each other tonight. I'd like you to stay with me until morning." She shifted her hand from his thigh to his penis, stroked it. "I've been alone here for a long time."

"What about your parties?" he asked.

"They're just . . . distractions. And I've also had the hope that I might find someone in attendance, someone I'd want to spend time with. But I never have. I haven't found anyone . . . until now."

"Emily," Clint said, "you don't think I'm going to stay here forever, do you?"

She laughed.

"Of course not," she said. "Just tonight, and then as many nights as you like while you're in the area."

"I see."

"So?" she said. "Shall we go down to the kitchen?"

"I'll just pull on my pants," he said.

She rose from the bed, grabbed a violet robe from a closet and slipped into it while he donned his trousers. He looked at his gun, which was hanging on the bed-post.

"You won't need it while you're here."

"Still . . ."

"Go ahead, then."

"I'll leave the holster," he said. "He took the gun and tucked it into his waistband, then followed her down to the kitchen.

They ate chicken, crackers and cheese, and drank wine. She talked about some of the time she'd spent there, and asked him about his recent time.

"We have a lot in common," she said, finally.

"How do you figure?"

"We spend a lot of time alone," she said. "Me here, and you on the trail."

"I have my horse."

"Of course."

"And that reminds me," he said. "If I'm going to stay the night, I'll have to see to him."

"There's a small leanto in back of the building," she said. "You can put him there and feed him. He'll be safe."

"I won't be long."

"I'll clean up here," she said. "Meet you back in the bedroom?"

"I'll be there."

Chapter Twenty

Clint went outside, walked Eclipse around to the leanto Emily had mentioned, unsaddled him and rubbed him down. There were some oats there, enough to satisfy the big Darley until morning.

"Get some rest, big fella," he said. "I'll see you in the morning."

He walked back around to the front of the lighthouse, stopped before going up on the porch. The moon was full, and he was able to see footprints on the ground. Someone had been near the building recently—a matter of hours. He looked around, didn't see or feel anything, and went back inside.

He looked around on the first level, saw that the kitchen was clean, went to the parlor. He saw nothing, was about to go upstairs when he looked at the sofa. There seemed to be the imprint of a body on it, as if someone had sat there recently.

Someone had been inside the building.

He went back upstairs to the bedroom.

***

"What are you saying?" Emily asked. She had been waiting on the bed naked, but when he entered and told her what he'd found, and what he thought, she grabbed the sheet and pulled it up to cover herself.

"I think someone was near the lighthouse," he said, "and even inside. Who else has a key?"

She remained silent.

"Ah," Clint said, "this is a secret, is it? A boyfriend, maybe?"

"No," Emily said, "no boyfriend. Do you know Janet Evans?"

"I do," he said. "She's my landlady."

"Ah," Emily said, "Well, whatever you do, don't tell her you spent the night here. She doesn't like me very much."

"What does she have to do with a key?"

"Her niece, Billie?"

"I've met her, too," Clint said. "She's not a very cooperative young lady."

"Oh, she's all right," Emily said. "She comes around here quite a bit. I like her, and she likes me."

"I see. So . . ."

"Yes," Emily said, "she has a key."

"And she's the only one?"

"Yes."

"So she might have been in here while we were in the bathtub."

"She's coming to terms with being a young lady," Emily said. "She's pretty, and men like her."

"I know," Clint said, "I was a target or her charms."

"Ah, and did you give in?"

"I didn't," Clint said. "She's still too much of a child."

"Not for much longer, I'm afraid," she said.

"Well," he said, sitting on the edge of the bed, "I also saw footprints left by men's boots."

She sat up straighter, held the sheet more tightly.

"That's not good."

"Have you been having trouble with anyone?"

"I've noticed three men watching me," she said.

"Watching you, or the lighthouse?"

"Both, actually," she said.

"How long?"

"About a week."

"Have they ever come this close?"

"Not to my knowledge."

"When I met Billie, she was being chased by three men on the beach," Clint said. "Was that them?"

"Probably."

"What's this about?"

"I'm not sure," she said.

"Do you think they might want to rob you?" he asked. "Has the lighthouse ever been robbed?"

"No," she said. "What would they steal? The lens?"

"Maybe."

"There's nothing they could do with it."

"Then what else might you have in here that they'd want?" he asked.

"I don't know."

"Have you talked to the police?"

"I don't go to town."

"Do you have a gun?"

"I have a rifle."

"And do you know how to use it?"

"I can hit what I shoot at," she said. "From eight-nine feet up I can probably hold off three men, but . . ."

"But what?"

She stopped holding the sheet so tightly to her.

"I didn't invite you back here just to show you the lens, and sleep with you. I was hoping I could persuade you to help me."

"In what way?"

"Maybe find out who they are," she said. "And what they want? Keep them away from me?"

"So that's what this is about?"

Now she dropped the sheet, so she was naked again. She leaned back against the bedpost, let one hand fall down between her legs.

"Not entirely."

He watched as she probed herself and grew wet.

"You know, in the end you really don't remind me of my husband, at all."

"Oh? How so?"

She tapped her pussy and said, "It's in the way you eat."

Chapter Twenty-One

By morning he was more exhausted than rested.

When he woke, Emily's leg was over his, and her arm was across his chest. He removed them gently, without waking her. When he got out of bed he looked down at her, lying naked on her belly. He traced the line in the center of her back until it disappeared between the glorious orbs of her big beautiful butt.

He felt his cock starting to stiffen again, just from looking at her, so he looked away. He decided to go downstairs and get cleaned up, maybe start some breakfast for her, before her body dragged him back into bed.

They had made love for most of the night, had probably only slept an hour or two. But he didn't want to stay in bed much longer, he wanted to start the day. From the look of the sun over the bay, it was probably close to nine a.m.

He went into the room where the bathtub was, found that there was also a sink with a water pump. He washed there, got dressed, went to the kitchen and put a pot of coffee on the stove.

He looked through her cupboards, found the makings for flapjacks, and had them cooking by the time she came down. She had her robe on, but it was off one shoulder, revealing much of her left breast.

"Cover up, Emily," he said, "or this table's going to have more than flapjacks on it."

"Ooh," she said, "is that supposed to be a threat? Why don't you just come back upstairs with me?"

"Oh, no," he said, "you kept me in bed all night, I'm not going to let you keep me in bed all day, too. Sit at the table. This morning I'll feed you."

She straightened her robe, tied it tightly, and sat at the kitchen table. He gave her a cup of coffee, then went back to the flapjacks. Eventually, he put two plates on the table.

"You got any molasses?" he asked.

"In that cupboard," she said, pointing.

He found the bottle, and put that on the table, as well, then sat across from her. He waited while she poured some molasses on her plate, then used it himself.

"This is very good," she said. "You can cook."

"Trail food," he said. "Bacon, beans, flapjacks when I have the makings."

"What are your plans for today?" she asked.

"Well," he said, "Last night you asked me to help you. I thought I'd do that."

"How?"

"I'll ride back into town and look for them," he said. "You can describe them, right?"

"Well, I've never seen them up close," she said, "but I can tell you something about them."

"Good," he said, "as much as you can."

"Then what?"

"I'll go looking for them," he said. "And maybe I'll talk to the police in town."

"The police," she said. "I don't really want to talk to them."

"Why not?"

"The Chief of Police," she said. "I don't like him."

"I can talk to him without mentioning you," he said. "I'll just tell him I saw them on the beach, chasing somebody."

"Billie?"

"I won't give her up, either," he said.

"And what will you do when you find them?" she asked.

"I'll talk to them," Clint said, "see what they want. I can probably persuade them to leave you alone."

"That would be great," she said. "I can't tell you how much I appreciate this."

"You can show me how much," he said.

"Definitely," she said, smiling. She ate her last bite of flapjacks and pushed her plate away. "Come back up to bed with me."

"No," he said, "I didn't mean now." He stood and carried the plates to the sink.

"Leave them there," she said. "I'll clean them later. You should probably get going."

"I'll go and saddle my horse," he said, "walk him around front."

"I'll get dressed while you do that," she said, "and see you out there."

***

He took Eclipse out of the leanto and saddled him, walked him around to the front. He stayed aware of his surroundings, but all he could hear was the water lapping at the shoreline.

Emily was waiting on the porch, once again wearing her work clothes. He joined her and kissed her. She gave him as good a description as she could of the three men. He also had the fact that he'd seen them himself, however briefly.

"I'll let you know if I can find out anything," he said.

"Come back tonight," she said.

"I've got a room in town," he reminded her.

"Oh, yes," she said, "Janet's place. I'm sure she'll be . . . worried."

"Probably not," he said. "While I'm looking for these men it might be better if I stayed in town."

"But you could come back for . . . a while."

He smiled and said, "I'll see you later."

She watched as he mounted up and rode back toward town.

Chapter Twenty-Two

Clint rode back into Pacific Grove, and suddenly it didn't feel as friendly as it had the day before. First three men were chasing Billie, and now they were watching Emily Fish and the lighthouse. What was going on in their heads?

He took Eclipse to the livery near his rooming house so the big guy could get a serious rubdown and feeding. From there he went to the rooming house, where he knew breakfast was over.

"You're late!" Janet told him as he walked in. "You missed breakfast."

"I understand that," Clint said. "I was kept overnight at—"

"You don't have to explain anything to me," she said, cutting him off. "As long as you pay for your room, you can sleep in it or not, as you please."

"Okay," he said. "Is Billie around? I'd like to talk to her."

"She came in late last night," Janet said, "and she didn't come down for breakfast."

"So she's in her room?"

"I don't know," Janet said. "All I know for sure is that she wasn't at the table this morning."

"Do you mind if I go and check?"

"As a matter of fact I do, yes," Janet said. "I won't have you in my niece's room. It's not decent."

"Well then, would you mind going to see if she's there?"

She glared at him and said, "I'm not your messenger. I have work to do. You'll just have to wait and see if she comes down. Excuse me."

If Janet's shoulder had been any colder it would have frozen him stiff. But he couldn't worry about that right now. He'd have to talk to Billie later. For now he was left with going to the police station to talk to the chief.

He left without telling Janet.

***

He entered the impressive two-story, brick police station building and presented himself at the front desk. The man standing at the desk was wearing Sergeant's stripes.

"Excuse me, Sergeant," he said.

"Can I help you, sir?"

"Yes, I'd like to see Chief Anderson."

"Do you have an appointment?" the Sergeant asked. "The Chief's a very busy man."

Clint almost asked the Sergeant if the Chief happened to be playing poker, but instead he said, "Would you mind asking him if he has time to see Clint Adams?"

"I'll check," the Sergeant said. "Please have a seat, sir."

There were benches there in the lobby, so Clint did as the Sergeant asked. But he didn't have to sit for long. The Sergeant returned just moments later.

"Follow me, sir," the Sergeant said. "The Chief says he can see you."

"Thanks."

He followed the Sergeant through the new station to the Chief's office. It was impressive, very large with several chairs and a sofa, and the Chief seated behind a huge expanse of desk.

"Mr. Adams," Anderson said, coming around from behind the desk. "Welcome to my station."

The two men shook hands.

"That'll be all, Sergeant," the Chief said.

"Yes, sir."

"Have a seat, Mr. Adams," he said, "and tell me what I can do for you."

Clint sat down and the Chief walked around his desk and took his seat.

"Can I get you anything?" he asked. "Coffee?"

"No, thanks," Clint said. "I'm fine."

"Then I'm all yours," Anderson said, with a wave. "What can I do for you?"

"I'm interested in three men who have been seen around town."

"What three men?"

"That's what I need to find out," Clint said. "I have a description of them. When I was riding into town I saw them chasing somebody on the beach."

"Who? Who were they chasing?"

"I can't say just yet," Clint said, "but I did manage to keep that person from being caught. Now I've heard those men are still around town, and they're looking for trouble."

"Well, we don't like trouble in Pacific Grove," the Chief said. "We frown on it. You give me their descriptions and I'll see what I can find out."

"I'd appreciate it." Clint gave the Chief the descriptions that he had, which he knew could apply to a lot of men, but three men together tended to be noticed.

"There's just one thing."

"What's that?"

"You don't intend to kill these men, do you?"

"Not at all," Clint said. "I want to find out what they're up to, and see if I can persuade them to change their minds-whatever it is."

"As long as there's no gunplay," Anderson said. "I won't stand for that."

"Understood," Clint assured him.

"Then we're on the same page," the chief said. "I'll be in touch."

"I'll find my way out," Clint said, shook hands with the chief, and left the office.

Chapter Twenty-Three

After Clint Adams left the station, Chief of Police Anderson called for his second in command, Lieutenant Briscoe.

"Sir?" Briscoe said, entering the office. "You wanted to see me?"

"Have a seat, Lieutenant."

Briscoe, at forty-one, was ten years younger than the Chief, and about fifty pounds lighter. At six feet, they were a match in height.

"I just had a visit from Clint Adams. Do you know who he is?"

"Well," Briscoe said, "there's a myth about a man with that name. They call him the Gunsmith."

"The man I met with today—and played poker with last night—is no myth."

"You mean he's real?"

"Real as you or me," Anderson said.

"Yes, but . . . surely the things they say about him can't be true."

"Even if they're half true, we have a situation on our hands."

"Just the fact that he's here would be a situation," the lieutenant said. "Is he looking for trouble?"

"He's looking for three men," Anderson said.

"To kill?"

"He says no."

"Do you believe him?"

"I don't really have a reason not to," Anderson said, "but I'd like to keep an eye on him, just in case."

"We can do that, sir. In fact, I could do it."

"No," Anderson said, "I need you to pick out your best man, have him follow Adams without being seen."

"Yes, sir."

"And let's remember his reputation."

"We'd have a problem if we were trying to follow him on the trail," Briscoe said, "but here in Pacific Grove I think we have the upper hand."

"I suppose," Anderson said, "that will depend on the man you choose."

"Yes, sir."

"And make it fast."

"Yes, sir."

Briscoe stood up and left the office. Anderson sat back in his chair, hoping they weren't heading for trouble.

As soon as Briscoe left the office, he knew the man he wanted. The Pacific Grove Police Department had two detectives. He went to the room where their desks were, found them both there. He studied them for a moment. Their names were Bailey and Steele. His first choice for this job was Steele. He was more athletically built, a few years younger, but both men were equally intelligent and good detectives.

"Steele!"

"Yes, sir?"

"Come with me." He looked at Bailey. "You'll be picking up any cases that come up for a couple of days. I have a special job for Steele."

"Yes sir."

He led Detective Steele to his office.

"Close the door," he said. "And have a seat."

Steele did as he was told and sat down.

"I have an important job for you . . ."

***

After leaving the police station, Clint decided to try his bartender contact, which was Jim at the Beach Grove Saloon.

It was too early for saloon hopping, so there were only a couple of patrons at the bar, and one of them was drinking coffee.

" 'mornin'," Jim said, as Clint approached. "Beer?"

"I'll have some coffee, if you've still got some."

"Comin' up."

He poured Clint a cup and set it down in front of him.

"What brings you in here so early?" Jim asked. "Lookin' for more poker?"

"Nope," Clint said. "Once was enough."

"Did you win?"

"I did okay."

"Then once was probably enough for them, too," Jim said.

"I'm looking for three men traveling together," Clint said, and gave Jim the descriptions he had.

"Those descriptions could match anybody," the bartender said.

"I know," Clint said, "but these three are together, and they're probably looking for trouble."

"Still not givin' me much," Jim said, "but hey, three of 'em? Maybe I'll see somethin'. Or somebody may have seen 'em."

"Just let me know," Clint said. "Any kind of sighting and I'll check it out."

"Okay," Jim said, "you got it."

"Thanks," Clint said. "Uh, don't send anyone to the rooming house looking for me. I'll check back here later to see if you've found out anything."

"Whatever you say."

Clint left the saloon.

Chapter Twenty-Four

His next move was to talk to Billie. But going back to the rooming house didn't seem an option, not with Janet Evans feeling the way she did. She needed time to cool off—or warm up.

There was only one other place he could think that Billie might be. If he was wrong then he was riding out there for nothing, but he didn't seem to have another option. Sitting around town and waiting for the three men to walk by him wasn't acceptable.

He went to the livery.

***

When the knock came at the door of the lighthouse, Emily ran to it, thinking it would be Clint. It wasn't. It was Billie.

"Why are you knocking?" Emily asked. "Lose your key?"

"No," Billie said, "the last time I used it I—well, I wanted to make sure he wasn't here."

Emily smiled.

"So that was you last night."

"Yes."

"Come on in."

They entered the lighthouse and went to the kitchen. Emily made them tea.

"So," Emily asked, "how much did you see or hear last night?"

"I didn't see anything . . ." Billie lied. She still had Clint Adams' naked body in her mind.

"But?"

". . . I heard a lot."

"Should I be embarrassed?"

"No," Billie said, "but I guess I should be."

"How long did you stay?"

"I was hiding behind the sofa when the two of you came out," she said. "As soon as I could, I left."

"Where did you go?"

"Where else?" Billie said. "I went home."

"And your Aunt?" Emily asked. "Did you . . ."

"What? Tell her?" Billie asked. "No, of course not. I didn't tell her anything."

That was good, Emily thought.

"Are you in love with him?" Billie asked.

"What? No, of course not," Emily said. "I barely know him."

"But . . . you were with him."

"Billie," she said, "you've told me that you've been with boys, and men . . ."

"Yes."

"Did you love them?"

"Well, no . . . but I'm learning," she said. "You know all about love, and sex."

"I thought I did," Emily said.

"You mean . . . he showed you more?"

Emily studied Billie, but didn't answer.

"Emily," Billie said, "you've always been truthful with me."

"I always tell you what I think you need to know, Billie," Emily said, "but there are some things that aren't your business. Just like there are some things in your life that aren't mine."

Billie pushed her half-finished cup of tea away.

"I've told you everything," she said. "I haven't held anything back."

Emily studied the young girl again, then said, "No, I guess you haven't."

"You're the only one I can talk to."

Emily reached her hand out and Billie took it.

"All right, then," she said. "Let's have some more tea and talk."

Clint rode up to the front of the lighthouse, dismounted and went to the front door. He knocked, waited, and then knocked again. Emily opened the door.

"Well, good afternoon," she said. "I didn't expect to see you again so soon."

"I've been looking for Billie," he said. "I need to speak to her. Is she here?"

"Yes."

"Can I come in?"

"I'll come out, first."

She stepped outside and closed the door.

"It was Billie who was inside last night."

"And," Clint said, "how much did she see?"

"She says nothing," Emily said, "but she heard us. She knows what we were doing."

"Is she . . . all right?"

"We've been talking," Emily said. "Apparently, I'm the only one she feels she can talk to . . . about everything."

"I see."

"I'll want to be there when you talk to her."

"That's fine with me," Clint said.

"All right, then," she said. "Let's go inside."

Chapter Twenty-Five

She took him to the kitchen, where Billie was sitting at the table.

"Billie, Clint's been looking for you," Emily said. "He wants to talk to you."

"Did you tell him . . .?" she asked.

"I did."

Billie looked away.

"I don't care about that, Billie," he said, sitting on her right while she was looking left. "I want you to tell me about those men who were chasing you."

Billie turned her head and looked at him.

"What about them?"

"I need to know who they are," he said.

"Why?"

"Well, they not only chased you," he said, "but they've been watching Emily, and the lighthouse. We're afraid they may be planning something."

Billie looked at Emily, who was leaning against the stove with her arms folded.

"You didn't tell me that," she said.

"I told you," Emily said, "some things aren't your business. I didn't want you to worry."

"But now we have an idea why they might have been chasing you," Clint said.

"Why?" Billie asked.

"To get your key."

Billie put her hand on her pocket.

"Did they say anything to you?" he asked.

"I was just walkin' on the beach when they yelled at me. 'Hey, girlie, get over here!' Well, I just started runnin'."

"Did they say anything else?" Clint asked.

"They just started yellin', 'get back here. And 'stop runnin',' and 'you're gonna get it.' "

"And you never saw them before?"

"No, never."

"Billie . . ." Emily said.

"I swear!" Billie cried. "I never seen them before. Not even in town."

Clint looked at Emily.

"I still don't have anything else," she said. "I just know they've been watching me."

"But why?" Billie asked. "Why would they watch you?"

"Obviously," Clint said, "they want to get into the lighthouse, and somehow they know that you have a key."

"I never told anybody I have a key," Billie said.

"Not your aunt?" Clint asked.

"Or a boy?" Emily asked.

"No!" Billie said. "I'd never tell my aunt. And I never told a boy nothin'!"

"Okay," Emily said, "okay, we believe you."

"Billie," he said, "I want you to show me the shortcut you take here. You walk, right?"

"Every time."

"And you get here faster than I do when I ride."

The girl nodded.

"Okay," he said, "I'm going back to town now. What about you?"

She shrugged.

"Do you have anything to do here?"

"She sometimes helps me clean the lens," Emily said, "but today's not the day."

"Then come back with me," he said. "Can my horse make it?"

"I think so."

"Good," he said. "Come on, let's go."

Billie stood up, walked to Emily and hugged her. Or rather, the woman hugged the girl warmly. Clint thought Emily and Billie had the relationship Billie should have had with her aunt.

Emily remained on the porch as they walked away, Clint leading Eclipse rather than riding him.

"Can I ride him?" Billie asked when they'd gone about half a mile.

"Can you ride him through the shortcut?"

"I think so."

"Okay," he said, "hop on."

He gave her a leg up and boosted her into Eclipse's saddle.

"Oh, wow," she said. "This is high up. He's so big."

"He is that," Clint said, "but after being up at the top of the lighthouse, it doesn't seem as high to me, any-more."

"That's different," she said. "The lighthouse ain't movin'."

"That's true."

They walked a while, and he just waited. He had the feeling she wanted to talk, but he was determined to let her come around to it herself.

"Clint?" she said. "Can I call you Clint?"

"You can," he said.

"Clint," she said, "I know a good spot where we can stop and have sex."

Chapter Twenty-Six

Clint stopped walking and turned to look at the girl.

"Billie," he said, "are you trying to shock me?"

"No," she said, with a wide innocent look, "I'm trying to get you to have sex with me."

"I have sex with women," Clint said.

"I'm a woman."

"Adult women," he said. "Not children."

She glared at him.

"I'm not a child!"

"Then stop acting like one," he said. "Were you embarrassed by what you heard last night?"

"I was," she said, "but I was also . . . excited."

"Just how much did you hear?"

She looked away.

"I heard—and saw—more than I told Emily."

"Is that a fact?"

"I saw . . . you."

"Me."

"Naked."

"Now it's my turn to be embarrassed."

Her hands touched the buttons of her shirt.

"If you'd let me undress, you'd be excited," she said. "I'm sure of it."

"Billie," he said, "don't get me wrong. You're a lovely young woman. But you're young. What you're suggesting . . . it wouldn't be right."

"Other men haven't had that problem."

"I'm not other men," he said. He pulled on Eclipse's reins. "We better get moving."

***

She directed him through the short cut, which took them across sand dunes, and through some brush. For the most part it was manageable for Eclipse. At one point Billie had to dismount, and they traveled single file for a while, but in the end she was able to mount again.

"Town is right around that corner," she said.

"This was a shortcut," he said.

"I use it a lot," she said.

"Does anyone else?"

"I don't know."

"Did those men chase you through it?"

"No," she said. "I was already on the beach when they started to chase me."

"That's good," Clint said. "We may have to use this shortcut again."

"How will you find out who those men are?"

"They can't hide forever," he said. "More than likely a bartender will see them somewhere."

"So what now?"

"Now I take you home," he said, "and you stay there."

"You should have left me at the lighthouse," Billie said. "I'd rather be there. It feels more like home."

"Just what is the problem between you and your aunt?" he asked.

"She hates me."

"Why do you say that?"

"Because it's true."

"Has she ever said that?"

"No."

"And how do you feel about her?"

Billie didn't answer.

"Isn't she your mother's sister?"

"She is."

"I can't believe she hates you, Billie," Clint said. "Maybe you should ask her."

"If you're gonna take me home," Billie said, "why don't you do it?"

Clint took Billie to the rooming house, waited out front until she went inside. He turned to mount Eclipse, but the front door opened and Janet came running out.

"Clint!"

He turned as she came down the steps.

"Where was she?"

"The lighthouse."

"With that woman!"

"Yes."

Janet folded her arms.

"Look," Clint said, "I don't know what your problem with Emily Fish is, and I don't care. But I do care about your problem with Billie."

"That's none of your—"

"She thinks you hate her!"

"What?" Janet looked stunned. "I don't hate her. That's ridiculous."

"Then what's the problem, Janet?"

She seemed to take a moment to look inside herself before focusing on him, again.

"I thought—I thought *she* hated *me*."

"Then the two of you have a lot to talk about, don't you?" he asked.

Chapter Twenty-Seven

After leaving Billie at the rooming house, Clint thought of somebody else who might have information for him.

He left Eclipse out in front of the Courier office and walked in, finding the editor, Charles Ferguson, hard at work.

"Change your mind about that interview?" Ferguson asked.

"Maybe."

"What can I do to change that maybe into a yes?" the editor asked.

"Answer some more questions?"

"Come on into my office," Ferguson said.

They went inside, Ferguson taking a moment to wipe as much ink from his hands as he could, on a towel.

"Drink?" he asked. "I've got a bottle of whiskey here."

"A small one," Clint said.

"Comin' up."

Like most roll top desks Clint had seen in his lifetime, this one had a whiskey bottle in a bottom drawer.

Ferguson took it over, grabbed two glasses and poured two fingers into each.

"There ya go," Ferguson said.

They both drank.

"What's on your mind, Mr. Adams?"

"Are you the one who started calling Emily Fish 'the Socialite Keeper'?" Clint asked.

"No," Ferguson said, "that was done in a Monterey newspaper . . . but I did jump on the bandwagon soon after."

"Is she wealthy?"

Ferguson frowned.

"I don't know."

"Aren't women who are called socialites usually wealthy?" Clint asked.

"I believe," Ferguson said, "the phrase means they're . . . social. Whether or not they're wealthy . . ."

"Do you think she has anything in that lighthouse that's . . . valuable?"

Ferguson frowned.

"Why are you asking me this?"

"Apparently there are three men watching her who are interested in getting into the lighthouse," Clint said. "They must think there's something of value in there."

Ferguson poured himself another drink, held the bottle out to Clint, who shook his head.

"There's a . . . story," the editor said, "maybe a myth . . . well, myth is a strong word. It hasn't been going on long enough to be a myth, but . . ."

Clint decided to wait, and let the man get to the point himself.

"Gold."

"What?"

"It's said that there's gold in the lighthouse."

"Gold?" Clint said. "I didn't see any gold."

"Did you see every inch of it?"

"Well, no . . . how much gold, exactly?"

"I don't know," Ferguson said, "perhaps enough to interest three men, though."

"I didn't think . . . that never occurred to me," Clint said.

Ferguson shrugged.

"Might be something else, but you asked me what I'd heard."

"Right." Clint stood up. "Thanks, Mr. Ferguson."

"How about that interview?"

When this is all over," Clint said, "I'll stop in before I leave town."

"For an hour?"

"Thirty minutes."

"Forty.

"Thirty."

"Sold," Ferguson said. "Thanks."

Clint left the newspaper office.

***

Detective Paul Steele picked Clint Adams up coming out of the Courier office.

He'd been looking for him all morning, was worried that he wasn't going to be able to do the job he'd been given by the lieutenant.

Now, as he followed Clint, he wondered where he was going and what he was up to? Why did the Lieutenant and—by assumption—the Chief want him followed? Were they just worried that he was going to cause trouble?

He was told to follow the Gunsmith, to keep out of sight, and report back on what the man did and who he saw. So far all he knew was that the Gunsmith had been to the newspaper office, maybe to talk to the editor. Later he could go back and find out what that was about.

The Gunsmith was walking his horse, and looked as though he was strolling, with no idea where to go. Steele stayed across the street, walking close to the storefronts, ignoring people when they greeted him.

Come on Mr. Gunsmith, he thought, pick someplace to go and go there.

Chapter Twenty-Eight

Clint wasn't sure what to do next.

He couldn't say that Emily had lied to him. She was under no obligation to tell him if she had gold or not. And he certainly hadn't asked her if she had any valuables in the lighthouse. Maybe that was a question he should ask, later.

He decided to go and see Jim at the saloon, see if he had any information for him on the three men.

***

Murrill had left Prado and Archer at the Whiskey Station Saloon with instructions to remain there. He couldn't afford to have them on the street with him. They'd be too noticeable.

He watched Clint Adams walk his horse to the Beach Grove Saloon, and leave it outside. Once he went inside the saloon, Murrill turned and headed for the Whiskey Station. With Adams in the Beach Grove, the lighthouse was theirs for the taking.

***

Detective Steele was watching Clint Adams very closely. For that reason he never noticed the other man watching the Gunsmith, also. Never noticed him turn and walk away as Adams entered the saloon.

He, however, remained across the street and watched the batwing doors of the saloon, waiting for Adams to come out again.

***

The saloon was still mostly empty. Jim had plenty of time to spend with Clint.

"I sent word out to some of the other saloons," he said. "I believe I have what you want."

"Three men?"

Jim nodded.

"Staying together, drinking together," he said.

"Where?"

"A small place called the Whiskey Station Saloon. I'll give you directions."

"Thanks, Jim."

"Do you need some back up?" Jim asked. "I have a Greener shotgun—"

"Thanks for the offer," Clint said, "but I think I can handle things."

"Be careful at the Whiskey Station," Jim said. "It's not like the rest of this town. In fact, it's in an area that's not like the rest of Pacific Grove. There are men there who might what to try you on for size."

"Well," Clint said, "I guess I'll feel right at home, then."

***

Clint followed the directions given him by Jim, which took him straight to the Whiskey Station Saloon. He saw what Jim meant by the area. This looked more like parts of town he'd seen in Tombstone and Abilene when he crossed their deadlines to the red light districts. Pacific Grove seemed such an idealistic town that he hadn't even wondered if it had a bad side.

He approached the Whiskey Station Saloon and listened. Although he had crossed a line, it was still quiet. There was no music, no loud voices. That might come when it got later, got darker. But as he approached the batwing doors and looked over them he could see that the saloon was more than half full.

He entered, and felt the eyes of the occupants turn to him. They studied him for a few moments and then, seemingly one-by-one, they turned their attention back to what they were doing—except for a few.

The kind of men who were in that saloon, one or two of them probably recognized him.

He walked to the bar.

"Beer," he said.

The bartender gave it to him, but then leaned in and said, "You better drink up and get out, Adams. There are too many men in here who wouldn't mind a try at your rep."

Clint sipped the beer, then set it down.

"Then maybe you can help me, and I'll leave."

"Whataya need?"

"Three men," Clint said, "always together. Maybe talking about something they were going to do."

"Talking?"

"Bragging."

The bartender laughed.

"Everybody in here brags."

"I'm talking about lately," Clint said.

The bartender rubbed his jaw.

"There were two men in here earlier, and then a third came running in," he said. "They talked and I heard one of them say something about a lighthouse."

"That's them."

"Don't tell me they believe that story about gold in the lighthouse?"

"I guess they do," Clint said. "When did they leave?"

"Just a little while ago," the bartender said.

"Thanks." If he used the shortcut, he might beat them there.

He turned to go to the door, found himself facing four men blocking his way.

Chapter Twenty-Nine

"Where ya goin', Gunsmith?" one of them asked.

All four were wearing sidearms in a manner that indicated they knew how to use them.

"Get out of my way," Clint said.

"Now, that ain't very friendly," the man said. "Me and my friends just wanna buy you a drink."

"That's okay," Clint said. "I don't need a drink."

"Come on," the man said. "This town is so damn borin'. You bein' here is the most excitin' thing that's happened in a long time."

"I'm happy I could be of help," Clint said, "but now it's time for me to be movin' on."

Clint started forward but the man held his left hand up, his right dangling by his gun.

"Not before we buy you that drink," he said. "We kind of insist."

Clint studied the man, and his three partners. None of them seemed particularly nervous. Generally, when facing more than one man, Clint was able to pick out the one or two weak links, but none of these men looked weak. In a case like this, he needed to key on the spokesman.

"Is this really necessary?" he asked. "Is this . . . whatever you think you're doing . . . worth dying over?"

"We ain't doin' nothin' but offerin' to buy you a drink," the man said.

"Well, if that's the case," Clint said, "I'll say thank you and come back for the drink later. Right now I have something I need to do."

He started forward again, but the man lifted his left hand.

"What now?"

"We're startin' to feel insulted."

"Look—what's your name?"

"Marsh."

"Look, Marsh, if this is going to end in gunplay, then let's get to it. I'm kind of busy."

"Four against one, Gunsmith," Marsh said. "Are you really that good?"

"You're about to find out."

"And you're not?" Marsh asked, with a crooked, uncertain smile.

"I already know," Clint said.

Marsh flexed his right hand. That was when Clint saw the weakness. It was not in the other three, but in the leader.

"I'm going to kill you first Marsh," Clint said. "Maybe after that your friends will back off and I won't have to kill any of them."

Marsh licked his lips but now he was sweating.

"Step aside, Marsh," Clint said. "Save your life, and the lives of your friends."

Marsh stared at him, licked his lips again, then moved his hand away from his gun. His friends followed, and they all stepped aside.

Clint moved toward the door, keeping his eyes on them.

"Go ahead, Gunsmith," the bartender said. Clint looked over and saw that the man was holding a shotgun. "I got your back."

"Thanks," Clint said, and went out the door.

***

"How are we gonna play this?" Prado asked.

They were about a hundred yards away from the lighthouse, in a stand of trees. They had watched the lighthouse from there before.

"Let's just go in the front door," Murrill said.

"And how do we do that?" Archer asked. "Knock?"

"Why not?"

"So?" Prado said. "Are we gonna do it now?"

"Let's go—" Murrill started, but Archer cut him off by grabbing his arm.

"Wait! Look!"

They all looked as Clint Adams rode up to the front of the lighthouse.

***

Clint took Billie's shortcut and pushed Eclipse. When he arrived he felt confident that he had beaten the three men there. Nevertheless, he rushed to the door and banged his fist on it.

"Well," Emily Fish said, when she opened it, "somebody's anxious to see me."

"Are you all right?"

"I'm fine."

"There's nobody inside?"

"Do you think I have a man here?"

"Maybe three men," Clint said, "holding a gun on you?"

"Ah," she said. "Well, no, I can assure you, I'm alone in here."

"Good," he said. "Can I come in, then?"

"Why not?" she asked.

He entered, watched as she closed the door.

"Why did you think there would be three men here?" she asked.

"They've been talking," he said. "Apparently, they're after your gold."

"My gold?"

"That's right."

She fell silent for a few moments, then said, "Maybe we should talk about this over coffee."

***

Detective Steele hastily got himself a horse when he realized Clint Adams was saddling his. He couldn't follow Clint, but he was able to follow his trail to the lighthouse. It took him through a shortcut he had never seen before.

He saw Clint's horse outside the lighthouse, hid himself and his horse and watched.

Chapter Thirty

Clint sat at the table while Emily got two cups and the coffee pot and put them on the table. She poured, then sat opposite him.

"There's no gold," she said.

"Took you a long time to come up with those three words," he said.

"I was just . . . thinking."

"Well," Clint said, "a lot of people think there's gold in here, and those three men are among them."

"And where are they now?"

"I thought they were on their way," he said. "That's why I rushed here."

"So they could be out there again, watching right now."

"They could be."

"They're not going to come now, though. Not while you're here."

"No," he said, "I'll have to go out and find them."

"What if they come here while you're out there?" she asked him.

"You said you have a gun."

"Yes, a rifle. But I can't go up against three men."

He sat back, stroked his jaw as he thought.

"They want to get inside, right?"

"Right."

"And once they get inside and have a look around, they'll realize there's no gold."

"Right again."

"Okay," Clint said, "so we need to give them a way to get inside."

"I can't just leave the lighthouse unattended," she said, "if that's what you're insinuating."

"No," he said, "not that."

"What then?"

"When is the last time you had a party?"

***

"Now what?" Prado demanded. "Is he comin' out?"

"Let's go," Murrill said, standing up. The other two men followed.

"Where?" Archer asked.

"Back to town."

"What for?"

"I need a beer," Murrill said, "and I want to know how he knew to come out here."

"He came to see the woman," Prado said.

"Yeah, but when he dismounted and got up on the porch he stopped and looked around."

"So?" Archer asked.

"He was looking for us."

"How could he know about us?" Prado said.

"That's what I want to find out."

***

After he explained his idea, she said, "Let me get this straight. You want me to have a kind of . . . what would you call it . . . open house?"

"That sounds good."

"A party for . . . everyone?"

"And anyone," Clint said. "We can put an open invitation in the newspaper."

"What about now?" she asked.

"What do you mean?"

"When you leave, I'll be alone," she said. "What if they see you leave and decide to break in?"

"I'm going to check the area first," he said. "If they're out there, I'll find them. If they're not, you should be safe for a while."

They walked to the front door.

"Where's your rifle?"

She pointed.

"Go and get it. I'll wait."

She left the room and came back with a Remington. He took it from her. It wasn't new, but he examined it and found it clean and in proper working order.

"Just keep it with you until I get back," he said, handing it to her.

"When will that be?"

"Later today," he said. "I'll check out of the rooming house and come here."

"I'm sure that will thrill your landlady."

"You know," he said, "at some point you'll have to tell me about you and her."

"There's not much to tell," she said, "but I'll save it for when you return."

"I'm going to search the area before I leave."

"I'll watch from the observation platform."

"I'll wave if everything's all right."

She grabbed his arm and he patted her hand before he went down the steps and mounted Eclipse.

***

He searched the entire area and finally came to a stand of trees that looked like an obvious place to watch from. He found some broken branches and—deeper

131

in—footprints. He followed the tracks to a place where there had obviously been three horses.

When he went back out from the trees, he waved to Emily to assure her that no one was presently watching her. From the observation platform she waved back.

He remounted Eclipse and rode to town, this time following the tracks left by the three horses.

***

Detective Steele remained where he was when Clint Adams came out with Emily Fish, who was holding a rifle. He watched as Clint started to search the area. Emily Fish went back inside, and in a few minutes appeared on the observation deck. If he remained where he was, the Gunsmith would find him. He had to withdraw.

He mounted up and rode to a point where the Gunsmith's search would not reveal him. He waited there, eventually saw three men riding toward town, who could only have come from the direction of the lighthouse.

Sometime later, Clint Adams also rode by, following the trail.

He gave Clint Adams a few minutes and trailed after him.

Chapter Thirty-One

The tracks led back to Pacific Grove, where they became obscured by others going in and coming out of town. He decided to check the Whiskey Station Saloon again.

"You're back for more trouble?" the bartender asked.

Clint looked around, didn't see Marsh and his friends.

"Where's Marsh?"

"He and his partners left soon after you did," the bartender said, sliding a beer over to Clint.

"And the three men who were talking about the lighthouse?" Clint asked. "Did they come back here?"

"No."

"Well, I know they were out at the lighthouse," Clint said. "They must have seen me arrive, and decided to simply ride back to town."

"Could be, but they didn't come here."

"Where else in town would someone who drinks here also go for a drink?" Clint asked.

"Well . . . there's Rachel's."

"What's Rachel's?"

"A cathouse."

Clint drank half his beer, then wiped his mouth with the back of his hand.

"Where is it?"

***

Rachel's was also over the deadline, in Pacific Grove's red light district. It was a two story wooden house with balconies and French doors on the second floor. In Tombstone or Abilene there would have been scantily clad girls up on those balconies, waving to men in the streets below, perhaps even baring a breast or two to entice them to come inside. It was either too early in the day, or Pacific Grove had laws against that, even in this section of town.

There was a white picket fence in need of repair. He left Eclipse by it and walked up to the front door. He had to knock twice before someone answered. It was a cute young redhead in a nightgown and robe, with a wild head of red hair, and sleepy eyes.

"It's way too early," she complained, "we ain't opened yet."

"I'm not interested in a poke," he said.

"Then whataya want?"

"Are there any men inside now?"

"I tol' ya, we're closed," she said, rubbing her eyes and staring up at him. This time, though, she saw enough to like what she saw. "But mebbe I can make an exception for you, honey." She let her robe open so he could see her hard little nipples poking at her nightgown. She was cute, all right. But he moved his eyes back to her face.

"Is there really a Rachel or is that just a name?" he asked.

"Rachel owns the joint," the girl said, "so she's real enough."

"Can I talk to her?"

"Oh, boy," she said, "if you wake Rachel up she'll shootcha just as soon as look atcha."

"When will she be awake?"

"We'll start settin' up in a couple of hours," she told him. "Comeback then, sweetie, and ask for me. I'm Jeannie. Don't let none of the other girls grab ya away from me."

"I'll be back," he promised.

"Oh, honey," she said, "you won't be sorry."

She backed up and closed the door, leaving him with one last sleepy smile.

He turned and walked back to Eclipse. He decided to go from there to the police station. He had something he needed to talk to Chief Anderson about.

Chapter Thirty-Two

"You've got a man following me," Clint said.

"Have I?" Chief Anderson replied.

"Don't play games with me, Chief," Clint said. "He may have been good at it inside your town, but out on the trail he's terrible."

Anderson frowned. He didn't like hearing one of his men spoken about like that. He also didn't like the fact that Clint had spotted the man.

"All right, I'm guilty," he said. "Guilty of having somebody watch your back."

"I wish I could believe that," Clint said. "However, even if that's why he was watching me, I doubt he would have done me any good."

Anderson rubbed the back of his neck. Clint had seen him do that during the poker game, when he drew cards and they weren't what he wanted. Apparently, the man's "tell" extended beyond the poker table.

"Just do me a favor," Clint said, "and pull him in before he gets hurt."

"I'll take care of it," Anderson said. Clint could tell from the redness of the man's face that somebody was going to hear about it when he left the station.

"Anything else? Did you find the three men you were looking for?"

"Not yet," Clint said, standing, "but I'm close."

"Just keep me informed . . . please."

"No problem," Clint said. "And please don't try putting anyone else on me."

Anderson held his hand up, but didn't say anything. He was too angry.

Clint left.

***

Anderson called his lieutenant in and told him to close the door.

"Sit!"

"Sir?" Briscoe said, sitting.

"That idiot you have following Adams was spotted."

"Chief, Steele is a good man—"

"Well, apparently not good enough," Anderson said. "Pull him in."

"I'll have to locate him—"

"Try looking right outside!" the Chief said. "Adams was just here."

"I see."

Briscoe stood up.

"Shall I put someone else on him?"

"No," Anderson said. "And you better take stock of your men. Apparently, the ones you think are your best are not!"

"Yes, sir."

"Now get out!"

Briscoe left the office and headed for the front door of the station.

*****

Clint crossed the street to where Detective Steele was standing, pretending to look in the window of a hat shop.

"I'm heading over to the newspaper office," he told the man.

"What?" Steele looked shocked.

"You better wait here," Clint went on. "I'm sure your boss will be out here any minute."

"I don't know what—"

Clint put his index finger in the detective's face and said, "Don't follow me!"

He turned and walked away.

Steele was about to follow him, but he saw Lieutenant Briscoe come out the front door of the station, look around and spot him. The man waved at him to come across the street, and waited with his hands on his hips.

***

Clint entered the office of the *Courier*, looked around for the editor, Ferguson. He didn't see him, looked through the glass to the man's office, didn't spot him there, either.

The only person he saw was an older man working the press, wearing a visor.

"Where's Mr. Ferguson?" he asked.

"Went out for coffee and a piece of pie," the man said. "He does that. Also to think."

"And where does he get his pie?"

The man pointed and said, "Go out the door, make a right and walk two blocks. It's a small café. Food ain't too good, but they got good pie."

"And how's the coffee?"

The man made a face.

"Too strong for my taste."

"Sounds perfect for me."

"If you like coffee that you could use to take paint off a wall."

"Love it," Clint said. "Thanks."

He went out the front door and made the right.

Chapter Thirty-Three

"He what?" Lieutenant Briscoe asked.

"Crossed the deadline," Detective Steele said. "He went to the Whiskey Station Saloon. Had a little run in with four gunmen."

"Did he kill them?"

"No," Steele said, "he talked them out of it."

"Talked them out of it?" Briscoe repeated. "The man with the biggest reputation as a fast gun talked four men out of a gunfight?"

"That's right."

"What was he doing there in the first place?"

"According to some people I talked to, he was looking for three men."

"And the four men he faced didn't include those three?"

"No."

Briscoe scratched his nose, leaned back in his chair. Steele was sitting across from him.

"What do I do, sir?" Steele asked.

"The Chief wants you to do nothing," Briscoe said. "Adams spotted you. We can't use you, anymore."

"I'm sorry—"

"Forget it," Briscoe said. "We're dealing with the Gunsmith. He's a legend, right?"

"So they say," Steele replied.

"Just stay out of the Chief's way until he cools off," Briscoe said.

"Yes, sir."

"That's all."

Steele stood and left the Lieutenant's office. Briscoe stood and looked out his window at the main street below him. Was the Gunsmith going to turn the street into a bloodbath before he left town?

***

Clint found the café with no problem, saw the editor sitting in the window. The man smiled when he saw him and waved him in.

"Sit, sit," he invited. "Have some pie."

Clint hesitated, glanced out the window. He made it a habit of sitting as far away from windows as possible, but as he looked around he didn't see too many other options. Apparently, everyone in town knew that this place had good pie.

Instead of taking the chair that faced the editor, he took the chair to the man's right, so he could look directly out the window.

"Is there a problem?" the editor asked.

"I don't like windows."

"Ohhh, I get it," Ferguson said. "Maybe we could move—"

"I just need to ask you for a favor."

"No pie?"

"No pie."

"Coffee? I've already got a second cup here."

"I'll take the coffee."

Ferguson righted the second cup, picked up the pot and poured. Clint could tell from the smell that the coffee was strong enough for him.

"Now what can I do for you? Uh, you don't mind . . ." He indicated his blueberry pie.

"No, go ahead and finish."

Ferguson stuck the pie in his mouth, revealing teeth that had already been stained blue, and said, "What's the favor?"

"Emily Fish has asked me to have you print an open invitation to a party at the lighthouse."

"An open invitation?" Ferguson asked. "So that means that anyone—"

"—right," Clint said. "Anybody can attend."

"That's a little unusual for the lady," the editor said. "Usually she's kind of . . . picky about her guests."

Clint shrugged.

"Hey, I'm just doing the lady a favor."

"I see."

"When's your next edition coming out?"

"Actually, tomorrow morning."

"Well, that sounds perfect," Clint said. "She said she'd like it to run as soon as possible."

"And what is the date of this party?"

"Well," Clint said, "since you're printing the invitation in the morning, why not make it tomorrow night?"

He sipped his coffee.

Excellent.

***

There was one person Clint felt he had to talk to, so they wouldn't be surprised by the invitation in the newspaper.

He entered the rooming house, found Janet cleaning the furniture in the livingroom.

"Is Billie here?"

"She's in her room."

"I have to talk to her."

"Go ahead."

"I—you don't want me in her room, right?"

She straightened up from what she was doing and looked at him.

"Believe it or not," she said, "I trust you. It's Billie I don't trust—but I think you can handle her."

"I won't be long," he said, "and then I'd like to talk to you before I leave."

"Sure," she said. "I'll be in the kitchen."

"Okay. Oh, uh, no more roomers?"

"No new roomers, no," she said.

He went up the stairs, made his way to Billie's room. The door was closed. He knocked.

"I'm busy, Aunt Janet," she called.

"Billie, it's Clint."

He heard her rush to the door and hurriedly open it.

"You're here!" she said. She grabbed his hand, pulled him in and closed the door. "I knew you wouldn't be able to resist for long." She started to unbutton her shirt.

"Whoa, hold on!" he said, waving his hands. "Don't do that, Billie. I'm here to talk."

"Talk first?"

"I'm here only to talk."

She dropped her hands from her buttons and her shoulders slumped. She walked to her bed and sat on it.

"What do you wanna to talk about?"

"Emily is having a party at the lighthouse." She brightened. "She is? When?"

"Tomorrow night."

"That's quick," she said. "Who's she inviting?"

"Everybody."

"What?"

"The whole town," he said. "The invitation will be in tomorrow's newspaper."

"Well, I'm glad you told me personally," she said. "I'll be there."

"That's what I wanted to talk to you about, Billie," he said. "I don't want you to come."

"What?"

Chapter Thirty-Four

"I don't want you to go to the party."

"Why not?"

"It could be dangerous."

"A party?" Billie said. "Emily's had lots of parties."

"Not like this," Clint said.

Billie studied him for a long moment, then nodded her head.

"Oh, I get it," she said. "You think those three men might be there."

"That's right."

"Then I have to be there," she said. "You need me."

"How do you figure that?"

"I'm the only one who's seen them," she said. "I can point them out to you as soon as they walk through the front door."

She was right. She was the only one who had ever seen the faces of the three men.

"I'll talk to your aunt," he said. "We'll need her permission for you to go."

"I don't need her permission!"

"Well," he said, "I do."

***

He found Janet where she said she'd be, in the kitchen. She was sitting at the table with a cup of tea.

"Would you like a cup?"

"No, thanks."

"Then coffee?"

"No."

"What is it you want to talk to me about?"

He told her what he had told Billie about the party at the lighthouse. And then he told her what Billie had said.

"She's just a silly girl," she said. "She's lying to you."

"No," Clint said, "the day I saved her from them she saw the three men. She can point them out."

"She'd be in danger."

"Can I sit?"

Janet nodded. He sat across from her.

"I won't let anything happen to her."

"You'll be spreading yourself a little thin, won't you?" Janet asked.

"Meaning?"

"I assume you made the same promise to Emily Fish."

"I did."

Janet shook her head.

"Janet, I need her."

She tightened her lips, then said, "Then I'm going, too."

"Why?"

"She's my responsibility," she said. "I won't let anything happen to her."

"Then that'll make two of us."

***

Clint agreed to let Janet and Billie make their own way to the lighthouse. He went to his room, collected his things, came back down to where Janet was waiting.

"So you're going to stay with her?" she asked.

"I'll be staying in the lighthouse," he said, "protecting it."

"You owe me money," she reminded him.

He took the money out of his pocket and paid her for his room.

"Thank you for the hospitality."

"You got more than that from me," she said.

"Janet—"

"Never mind, Clint," she said. "Just go and do what you have to do."

"I'll see you tomorrow night."

She didn't respond.

"You'll see us," Billie said, from the stairs. "Don't worry."

He nodded and left.

Chapter Thirty-Five

When he got back to the lighthouse he stowed his gear in a corner.

"Why don't you put it in my room?" Emily asked. "After all, you'll be sleeping there."

"I'll be sleeping down here, on the sofa," he said.

"Why?"

"To be on watch."

"You think they might try to break in tonight?"

"I don't know," he said, "but there's no point in being careless about it."

"I see what you mean," she said. "Well, you will be eating supper with me, right?"

"Definitely."

"Then I better get to the kitchen."

"I'm going to go up to the observation platform," he said. "Is that all right?"

"Yes," she said, "just don't touch anything while you're up there."

"I won't," he promised.

She was making noises in the kitchen while he went up the steps to the next level. It was daylight, so the lens wasn't lit. He stepped out onto the observation platform and walked around so he could see all sides. If they were being watched at that moment, he couldn't tell. He looked straight down when he got to the front again, and saw Eclipse. Realizing he had to take care of the horse he went back down.

"I'll be right back," he called to her. "I'm going to see to my horse."

"All right."

He went outside and once again took Eclipse around back to the leanto. He unsaddled him and brushed him down, then fed him.

"I know it's not much, big fella," Clint said, "but it's only for today. Tomorrow, I'll take you back to town."

The big Darley bobbed his head up and down and then went back to feeding.

Clint returned to the lighthouse.

"Are you hungry?" Emily called out.

"Actually, I am," he said.

"I made some lunch for us," she said, coming to the doorway of the kitchen. "Come on."

He went to the kitchen, saw that she had covered the table with food.

"I just realized something," he said, as they sat at the table.

"What's that?"

"You'll need food for the party tomorrow night," he said. "I should have arranged it while I was in town. I don't want to go back again tomorrow and leave you alone, but—"

"Don't worry about it."

"Don't tell me you have enough food for a party."

"I have enough food here for weeks," she said, "but not for a party. And I have a standing order with a restaurant in town. Once they read the newspaper tomorrow morning they'll send someone out here to take my order."

"That's handy," he said.

"So now we can just concentrate on eating," she said.

"Good," he said, "because I'm starved."

***

"There," Murrill said, "that's them."

"How'd you know?" Prado asked.

"I asked around," Murrill said.

"So what do we do?" Archer asked.

"We talk to them," Murrill said, "and get them on our side."

152

They were in the Beach Grove Saloon. Jim the bartender was leaning on the bar, waiting for more customers.

"Prado," Murrill said, "go to the bar and buy our friends some beers."

"Wha—"

"Just do it! Bring them to the table."

"Fine!"

Murrill and Archer walked over to the table where Marsh and his three partners were sitting.

"Hey, Marsh," Murrill said.

Marsh looked up, frowned.

"Do I know you?"

"Not really," Murrill said, "but I know you. I heard how the Gunsmith humiliated you and your boys, here."

The man growled something unintelligible and looked away. Murrill noticed their beer mugs were almost empty. At that moment Prado came over carrying four full mugs on a tray.

"Why don't you boys dig into these fresh ones," Murrill said, setting them on the table one at a time, "and we can all have a talk."

"Talk about what?" Marsh demanded.

"On how to get back at Clint Adams for what he did," Murrill said. "See, I have an idea."

Marsh grabbed a fresh beer and said, "You might as well sit down, then."

Chapter Thirty-Six

"What's your name?" Marsh asked.

"I'm Mitch Murrill. That's Prado and he's Archer."

Murrill didn't even hear it when Marsh told him the other men's names. It didn't matter.

"What's on your mind?" Marsh asked.

"I told you," Murrill said, "the Gunsmith. He deserves to get what's comin' to him."

"You kin say that again," one of the other men said.

"So what do you have against Adams?" Marsh asked.

"He did the same thing to us that he did to you," Murrill lied, "but there are four of you. I think you coulda took him."

"I think so, too," one of the other men said.

"Yeah, that's what I said," another said.

Murrill looked around the table. The other three were all nodding their heads, so it seemed like he had them. He looked at Marsh, wondering if he had him.

"You're the leader, ain't you?" he asked.

"So?"

"These three are lookin' to you," Murrill said, "just like Prado and Archer look to me."

"Are you sayin' the seven of us can take him?" Marsh asked.

"That's what I'm, sayin'," Murrill said, "only it can't look like seven against one, and it can't look like we ambushed him."

"So what do you suggest?"

"I've got an idea," Murrill said . . .

***

"Do you really think those three men will walk in here tomorrow night for the party?" Emily asked.

She was cleaning the table off after lunch, while Clint remained seated, drinking coffee.

"I think they'll probably walk in to take a look around," Clint said.

"And what will you do?"

"I'll see them," Clint said.

She turned away from the sink and looked at him.

"That's all?"

"Once I see them," he explained, "I'll know which one is in charge. And I'll probably take him aside and have a talk with him."

"You mean threaten him?" she asked. "Scare him?"

"I don't threaten people," he said. "I'm honest. I just tell them what's going to happen. If that scares him, then we're in business."

"And if not?"

"Then I'll probably have to do more," he said, "but at least I'll know who they are. They won't be able to hide anymore."

"Maybe," she said, "when you talk to him you could take him up to the observation platform. Show him what it looks like from eight-nine feet up—and what it might be like to fall from there."

"I like the way you think," he said. "That sounds like a great idea."

She wagged a finger at him and said, "Just don't let him touch the lens."

"Got it," he said, raising his coffee cup.

***

Later they were standing out behind the lighthouse, looking out at the water.

"It's beautiful," he said, "and quiet."

"I love it here," she said. "It's basically why I never go into town. It's too noisy."

"It's a lot quieter in Pacific Grove than a lot of towns I've been in."

She laughed.

"Well, I've never been to Tombstone or Abilene," she said, "but it's noisy to me. This," she waved her arms, "this is quiet."

"I can't argue with that."

"Do you want to walk along the beach?" she asked.

"With you? Sure."

"No," she said, "I have to go back inside. I can't just leave the lighthouse unattended. But you can walk. It's nice."

He looked up and down the beach, then over at Eclipse, who was standing calmly.

"Well, maybe just a little bit," he said, "but I won't go so far I won't be able to hear if you call."

"I'll be fine," she assured him.

He walked her back around the lighthouse and made sure she got inside safely, then went back around. He hadn't walked a beach since years ago in Mexico.

He didn't walk very far before he turned and headed back. He stopped and looked up at the lighthouse. He found it impressive from every angle. He hoped he was doing the right thing by having her host a party the next night. Hopefully, it would solve everything.

He walked back to the lighthouse.

Chapter Thirty-Seven

They sat on the sofa together with glasses of wine after Emily had made a delicious supper.

"It's a good thing I'm not going to be staying here long," he said. "I'd get fat from all this good food."

"Well," she said, "there is all the extra exercise I can offer you."

"Oh, you mean going up and down the stairs to take care of the light?"

"Yes," she said, "that's exactly what I meant."

He knew she wanted him to come to her bedroom with her, and it took all his will power to turn her down.

"We can't take the chance of something happening tonight when we're not ready," he said.

"I understand," she said. "Tell me, how did you get the editor of the newspaper to agree to run the invitation so soon?"

"Oh, he was easy," he said. "All I had to do was agree to an interview."

"Is that something you do a lot?" she asked. "Newspaper interviews?"

"No," he said, "I don't normally do them at all, so when this is over I'll expect you to really show me your appreciation."

"I already offered to do that tonight."

"Okay, we talked about that, already."

"Well then," she said, putting her wine glass down, "if you're going to stick to your guns—no joke intended—I'll just go to my room and turn in, after I check on the light."

"Want me to come up with you?"

"No," she said, "if you're going to resist my womanly charms, I don't want you in a small, confined space with me."

"Understood," he said, and remained on the sofa.

"Good night."

He watched her go up the stairs, kicking himself for not going with her.

***

Clint finished his wine and then went out onto the porch. He paused there and listened intently. If men were watching, they wouldn't be able to keep completely still or stay quiet for very long, especially if there were three of them. It just wasn't natural. When he was

159

satisfied that no one was out there, he went around the lighthouse to check in on Eclipse.

Back inside he saw that Emily had come down and left him a pillow and a blanket. He poured himself another glass of wine, only because there was no beer, then sat on the sofa between the pillow and the folded blanket.

****

"I don't get it," Prado said.

"What don't you get?" Murrill asked.

They were seated at a table in the Whiskey Station, with Archer, all with mugs of beer in front of them.

"Why bring Marsh and those other three into this?" Prado asked. "We ain't gonna share the gold with them, are we?"

"Hell, no," Murrill said, "we're just gonna have them help us get the gold—and get rid of Adams."

"And then you think they're just gonna walk away?" Archer asked.

"If they kill Adams, they'll happily walk away," Murrill said. "If they don't kill him . . . well . . ."

"They'll be dead," Prado said.

"Right."

"And we'll have the gold," Archer said.

"Right again."

"What about that woman?" Prado asked.

Murrill looked at him.

"You want her, don't you?" Murrill asked.

Prado grinned.

"Not for long."

"No problem, then," Murrill said. "She's all yours once we have the gold."

"Hey," Archer said.

Murrill looked at him.

"What about me?" Archer demanded.

"Fine. You can have a turn, too."

Archer smiled.

"And what about you?" Prado asked.

"If I want a woman," Murrill said, "I'll just go to Rachel's."

"Them women ain't like her," Prado said. "They're just whores."

"All women are whores," Murrill said, "in one way or another."

"So you don't like women?" Archer asked.

"Just the opposite," Murrill said. "I really like whores." He finished his beer and stood.

"Where you goin'?" Prado asked.

"Like I said," Murrill answered, "I like whores. If you need me, I'll be at Rachel's."

As Murrill left, Prado said to Archer, "How about another beer."

"If you're buyin'."

"Sure," Prado said, "if you're goin' to the bar to get 'em."

"Deal."

Chapter Thirty-Eight

The next morning there was a knock at the front door while they were having breakfast. Clint held his hand out to Emily as she started to stand, and went to the door himself.

"Oh, uh, hello," a skinny young man said, looking confused. "I was looking for Mrs. Fish? I saw the invitation in the newspaper this morning, and figured she'd be needin' some food."

"It's all right, Clint," Emily said, coming up next to him, "this is Johnny, from the Range Restaurant in town. Come on in, Johnny. I've got a list for you."

"Sure, Mrs. Fish." He slipped by Clint nervously, saying, " 'scuse me."

She showed him into the kitchen, where they discussed her list for a few moments before she walked him back to the door.

When he was gone she turned to Clint and said, "You scared him, answering the door with your gun on, like that."

"It's the only way I ever answer the door," he said. "Besides, he wasn't scared, he was jealous. That young fella is in love with you."

"Don't be silly," she said. "He's almost young enough to be my son."

"Doesn't matter," he said. "Men sixteen to sixty will fall in love with you. Don't you know that?"

"I have to clean the lens today," she said. "I don't have time for your fantasies."

"Hey," he said, "I want to take a chair up to the observation platform. Is that okay?"

"You want to sit out there?"

"Yeah," he said, "get kind of used to the heights, you know? I mean, if I'm going to take anyone else out there."

"Oh, I get it," she said. "Well, sure. Take a chair up. There's a beautiful view if you can relax long enough to look at it."

"Which way?" he asked. "Over land or sea?"

She shrugged. "Both."

"All right, then."

She collected her cleaning fluid and rags, and he followed her up the stairs carrying a wooden chair.

For the remainder of the morning he sat and watched her clean, took the chair to the other side and sat and looked out at the water.

When she was finishing up he was sitting out front, looking out over the sand and trees, when he saw a buckboard coming down the road.

"Wagon coming," he called, standing up and leaning on the rail. He was a little more comfortable up there, now.

She came out and stood next to him.

"That's Johnny, with the food." She looked at him. "Can you go down and help him carry it in?"

"He wants to see you," he said. "Aren't you afraid I'll scare him?"

"I don't want to see him."

"Why not?"

She looked away.

"You've made me self-conscious."

"You know," he said, "you don't come across very shy."

"Maybe not here," she said, "and not with you. But with other people . . ."

"Then how did you become the Socialite Keeper?"

"I told you," she said, "I'm comfortable as long as I'm here, in the lighthouse."

Down below the buckboard pulled to a stop in front of the lighthouse.

"Please?" she asked.

"Fine," he said. "I'll go down and help the young man carry in your groceries."

"Thank you."

He turned and went down the stairs, getting to the bottom by the time Johnny knocked on the door again.

"Oh," the young man said, "uh, it's you."

"Again," Clint said. "Come on, I'll help you carry the boxes in."

"Yeah, okay."

They went back and forth from the buckboard to the kitchen until they had all the boxes on the kitchen table.

"Are you always the one who delivers the groceries?" Clint asked.

"Yah," Johnny said, "I, uh, sort of volunteer."

"You like Emily—Mrs. Fish, right?"

"I, uh—" The boy shuffled his feet. "She's really pretty."

"Yeah, she is." They stood there awkwardly for a moment. "Does she pay you?"

"Huh? Oh, no, I get paid by Mr. Peterson. I just . . . well . . ."

"She's upstairs, cleaning the lens."

"Oh."

"I'll tell her you, uh . . . I'll tell her you delivered the groceries."

"Okay."

He walked the boy to the door, watched him climb up into the seat and start the buckboard back up the road. Then he looked up 89 feet and saw Emily looking down at him. She smiled and waved.

Chapter Thirty-Nine

Murrill woke the next morning with the whore, Lily, lying with her arms across his chest, and her big heavy breasts pressed against him. He ran his hand down her back to her big ass and slapped it.

"Hey!"

"Time to wake up!" he said. "Time to wake me up. You know how I like to wake up."

She looked over at him, groggy with sleep—or lack of it. He kept waking her up all night to do it again.

"Come on, Lily," he said, "I'm hungry, and I got people to see."

She sat up, asked, "What people have you got to see?" and then stretched. Her arms straight over her head lifted up those big tits and made the brown nipples look right at him. She was only about ten pounds away from being a chubby whore, but he didn't mind. Staring at those big tits, his cock was already starting to get hard.

"Lily!"

'All right, all right," she said. "At least lemme wake up!"

"Wake up with my cock in your mouth!" he snapped.

"You sweet talker, you," she said. She leaned down over him and took him in her mouth, and he was fully hard by now. As she started to suck he put his hands on the back of her head.

"That's it," he said, "wake me right up!"

***

"Why can't we go to the party?" Marsh asked.

"If the four of you walk in there and Adams sees you, there'll be trouble."

"Ain't that what you want?"

Murrill and Marsh were sitting alone at a table in the Whiskey Station. Murrill had gone there right from breakfast. The Whiskey always opened early, for most of their customers started drinking early.

Marsh's partners were standing at the bar, while Prado and Archer were sitting together, drinking beer.

"Yeah," Murrill said, "but not right in the middle of a room full of people. I want it to happen out in front— or on the beach."

"Never had a gunfight on a beach," Marsh said.

"Well, if you get him out there, make sure you spread out in front of him," Murrill said. "We don't want him to see me and my boys coming up behind him until it's too late."

"Right."

"He's gonna be sorry for what he did to you, Marsh."

"You got that right," Marsh said. "Real sorry."

"I'll see you and your boys out there," Murrill said. "Make sure it's a couple hours after the party, but well before it gets dark. Right?"

"I understand."

"Okay," Murrill said, "have another beer with your partners."

Marsh went back to the bar, while Murrill rejoined Prado and Archer.

"I just thought of somethin," Archer said.

"What?" Murrill asked. "Like maybe you should have something for breakfast besides beer?"

"No," Archer said, "like maybe there'll be somebody from the police department at this party. Did you ever think of that?"

"Think of it?" Murrill asked. "I'm counting on it."

***

For the rest of the afternoon Emily was in the kitchen preparing food for the party. When Clint offered to help she shooed him away.

"I don't offer to help you clean your guns, do I?" she asked.

That was a good idea. So he decided to go back up to the observation platform, sit there and clean his guns. By the time the weapons were properly cleaned and re-assembled, he was very comfortable up there. And Emily had been right. From every direction the view was beautiful.

***

"Clint! Clint!"

She called several times before he heard her. He came down, carrying his rifle.

"You called?"

"Now I do need your help," she said.

"In the kitchen?" he asked.

"Yes," she said, "and you won't need the rifle."

He set the rifle down and followed her.

"I need you to taste a few things," she said, looking down at the food that covered the table. "I want them to be just right."

He studied her for a moment. "I'm sure everything will be just as right as you are, Emily."

She looked up at him and smiled.

Chapter Forty

When people began to arrive, Clint realized that some of them had walked from town. He wondered if they'd taken Billie's short cut. Perhaps she wasn't the only one to use it, after all.

Others came in buggies and buckboards, or on horseback. He met the town doctor, the undertaker, some of the business owners like Peterson who owned the general store, and Mrs. Baily who owned the dress shop.

When Billie arrived, he was surprised to see her wearing a dress. She had a ribbon in her hair and was looking very pretty.

"You look beautiful," Clint said to her.

"Yes, you do," Emily said. But Billie didn't look happy. "What's wrong?"

Emily knew what was wrong a moment later, when Janet walked in.

"Hello, Janet," she said.

"Emily."

"Hello, Janet," Clint said.

"Hello, Clint."

"I was just telling Billie how nice she looks," Clint said. "You look lovely, as well."

"Thank you."

"Please," Emily told her, "help yourself."

"Thank you," Janet said.

Janet saw someone else she knew, another woman from town who had a hat shop, and went over to talk to her.

"I'm sorry," Billie said, "she wouldn't let me come alone."

"It's all right," Emily said, putting her hand on Billie's shoulder. "I'm just glad you're here."

Billie looked around and said, "I don't see those men here, yet."

"They'll probably wait until we're good and busy," Clint said.

"I'll watch the door," she promised.

"Okay," Clint said, "but do it so that when they come in they won't see you."

"Yes, sir."

"And get something to eat, first."

Billie nodded, then said to Emily, "You look real pretty."

"Thank you."

Emily was wearing a party dress and, like Billie, had a ribbon in her long hair.

"She's wrong, you know," Clint said.

"What?"

"You don't look pretty," he said. "You look beautiful."

She smiled and said, "Thank you."

***

Eventually, Chief-of-Police Anderson made an appearance, and fawned over Emily Fish like most of the men did.

"You're looking as lovely as ever," he told her.

"You're very kind, Chief," she said. "Please, help yourself to some food and drink."

"I hope we'll have time to talk later?" he asked.

"I'm sure we will," she said.

The Chief nodded to Clint and walked into the kitchen.

"My God, I can't stand that man," she said.

"Why's that?" Clint asked.

"He just makes me feel . . . slimy," she said, hugging her upper arms.

She looked around the room, filled with people now, eating her food, talking to each other.

"Is this how it usually is?" he asked.

"How do you mean?"

"The men fawn all over you," he said, "and the women ignore you and talk to each other."

"Pretty much."

"Why do you have these parties, then?"

"Well," she said, "you know why I'm having this one. Actually, what you don't know is that the Socialite Keeper hadn't had a party like this in some time. I'd grown pretty tired of them."

"I see."

"Looking around," she said, "I can see nothing's changed. The men and women from town treat me much the same way as they ever did."

"I'm sorry I made you do this, then—"

"Oh, you didn't make me do it," she said. "I agreed, because you said it might help."

"I hope it does," he said. "I'd hate to have you go through all this for nothing."

"I better mingle," she said, touching his arm. "Just rescue me if the Chief manages to corner me, will you?"

"You bet I will."

He looked around as she walked away, spotted Billie sitting in a corner, eating from a small plate and watching the front door. It was a good place for her, where anyone coming through the door wouldn't be able to see her.

He looked at the door himself now, wondering when they'd be putting in an appearance? There was no way they'd be able to resist this chance to get a look inside the lighthouse.

Chapter Forty-One

The editor of the *Pacific Grove Courier*, Charles Ferguson, was the next to arrive, and smiled when he saw Clint standing inside the door.

"Mr. Adams," he said, "a pleasure to see you."

"And you." Clint noticed the man was carrying a pad. "Here to party, or work?"

Ferguson lifted the pad up and said, "A little bit of both, I'm afraid. And where is our lovely hostess?"

"She's around," Clint said, "mingling."

"Good for her," Ferguson said. "I wish she'd come to town once in a while."

"Why?" Clint asked. "Do you think she needs friends?"

"I think," Ferguson said, "that her unwillingness to leave this lighthouse feeds the stories about there being gold inside."

"And where was this gold supposed to have come from?" Clint asked.

"There was a strike here some years ago—ten, twelve—that petered out pretty quickly. But some people got rich off of it."

"And was she here ten or twelve years ago?"

"No."

"Then why would she have any gold from that strike?" Clint asked.

"There are people who won't ask themselves that question," Ferguson said. "They will only ask themselves 'how do I get my hands on that gold?' "

"And that's why we're here," Clint said.

"I'll go and mingle, as well," Ferguson said. "I don't want to distract you from your task."

"Thanks."

Clint was watching the editor move into the party when he felt someone yank on his left arm.

"Clint," Billie hissed urgently, "it's them!"

He turned and looked at the door, saw three men coming in together.

"Are you sure?"

"Yes," she said. "They chased me that day."

"All right," he said, "go and hide."

"Hide?"

"I don't want them to see you."

"Where should I hide?" she asked. "Up by the light?"

"No, I'll be going up there," Clint said. "One of the bedrooms."

"I'm at a party and I have to hide in a bedroom?"

"Billie—"

"All right, all right," she said, raising her hands. "I'll go."

She slid away and he turned his attention to the three men—who, oddly enough, were approaching Clint. The man in the lead—who must have been the leader—was actually smiling at him.

"Hello, Adams," he said. "I heard you were looking for us."

"Where would you have heard that?" Clint asked.

"I forget," the man said. "A bartender, probably."

"And did he say why I was looking for you?"

"No," the man sad. "I figured you'd tell me that. My name's Mitch Murrill."

"And these two?"

"They're my friends," Murrill said. "They're names don't matter." Murrill turned to them. "Why don't you boys go and get something to eat?"

And look for gold, Clint thought.

The two men moved off.

"Is there someplace we could go to talk?" Murrill asked. "Maybe alone?"

"Would you like to see the light?" Clint asked.

"All the way up there?" Murrill asked. "Hey, that'd be interestin'."

"Let's go."

"Lead the way."

That wasn't likely, though. Clint wasn't about to let a man with a gun follow him up the stairs. When they reached the stairway he stopped and stepped aside.

"After you."

"You don't trust me?"

"I'm just careful."

"Sure, why not?" Murrill said, and started up the steps.

When they reached the top Clint said, "I'm going to have to ask you not to touch the light."

Murrill showed the palms of his hands.

"In fact, why don't we step outside?"

"Why not?" Murrill asked. "I don' think you have a reason to throw me off—yet."

Out on the observation platform Murrill stood at the rail, with both hands on it, looking out.

"Wow, what a view," he said. "I guess you could see us watching the lighthouse from here, huh?"

"Chasing the girl, watching the lighthouse," Clint said, "there's no gold, you know."

Murrill turned to look at Clint. He leaned back against the rail and folded his arms. He was a rangy man in his 30's, and from the way he wore his gun—and cared for it, since it appeared clean—he was familiar with how to use it. Clint wondered about the other two men.

"Gold?" Murrill repeated. "What gold?"

Chapter Forty-Two

"Come on, now," Clint said. "Why else would you and your friends be interested in this lighthouse?"

"It's a beautiful thing."

"And why would you be chasing a teenage girl along the beach?"

"Were we?"

"You were," Clint said. "I saw you, remember?"

"Well," Murrill said, "she's a pretty little gal, don't you think?"

"And young."

"Have you talked with her?"

"Yes, several times."

"Then you know what a tease she is," Murrill said. "She teased my friend until he broke. If you saw us running, then you know that he was chasing her, but I was chasing him. I was trying to help her."

Clint thought back, but in his mind, he could only see the three men running together on the beach. It was a good story, but he didn't believe Murrill for a moment.

"You know," Murrill said, "I'm not as dumb as people think I am."

"Or maybe," Clint said, "you're not as dumb as you'd like people to think you are."

Murrill smiled.

"Either way," Murrill said, "do you think I'd believe a story about gold in a lighthouse from a strike that went bust ten years ago?"

"Then why would you and your friends be watching this lighthouse?"

"I am an admirer," Murrill said.

"Of?"

"Well," Murrill said, "the lady is pretty, but I admire lighthouses. Me and my friends are gonna ride up and down the coast and look at 'em."

"Starting with this one."

"Right."

"Then why not just knock and ask to see it," Clint asked, "like I did?"

"Because of the kid," Murrill said. "My friend Tom Prado and young Billie had a . . . relationship, and then a fight. Because of that, there was no way Mrs. Fish would let us in here."

Clint stared at Murrill for a while and then said, "You think I'm going to believe that you fellas just wanted to get a look inside this lighthouse because you're 'admirers.' "

"Well, I am," Murrill said. "My friends were just along for the ride."

"And now that you've seen the inside, you'll be on your way?"

"That's right."

"And what about Prado?" Clint asked. "Is he going to leave Billie alone?"

"Of course," Murrill said. "We'll be gone."

"That remains to be seen."

Murrill laughed.

"I swear," he said, spreading his hands apart, "by tomorrow mornin' we'll be on our way."

"Maybe," Clint said, "we should get back to the party."

Murrill stared over the railing.

"Looks like some more guests arrivin'."

Clint also looked down. He saw Marsh and his three friends walking toward the lighthouse. They were wearing their guns, and walking with purpose.

"Now what are they doing here?" he said.

"The thing in the newspaper did say anyone was invited," Murrill remind him.

***

By the time they reached the main floor, Marsh was shouting from outside.

"What's going on?" Emily asked.

"That's what I'm going to find out."

"Adams!" Marsh called. "You better get out here! Or we'll come in! You ain't gonna like that."

Emily looked around, spotted Chief-of-Police Anderson and rushed over to him.

"Can't you do something?" she demanded.

"About what?" he asked. "Nothing's happened yet."

"But it will," she said, "if Clint goes out there."

"Then I'd have to study the situation," he said, "and make an arrest, if it's warranted."

She went back to Clint.

"You're not going out there, are you?"

"You don't want them coming inside."

"This is crazy," she said. "Who are they?"

"Just the fellas I had a little run in with the other day," he said. "I guess they've gotten their nerve up, somehow."

"Clint—"

"Just stay inside." He looked at Anderson. "Keep everyone inside, Chief."

Chapter Forty-Three

Clint went to the door and stepped out onto the porch.

"Mr. Marsh," he said. "You and your friends come to the party?"

"To hell with your party," Marsh said. "You humiliated us the other day. We're here to teach you a lesson."

"Right here?"

"No," Marsh said, "on the beach."

"A gunfight on the beach?" Clint asked. "That will be a first."

"Meet us there in five minutes," Marsh said, "or we're coming inside."

He turned and walked around the lighthouse, followed by his other three men, still nameless to Clint.

Clint felt someone behind him, looked to see Billie standing there.

"You're supposed to be inside."

"Those three men are inside."

"Speaking of that," Clint said, "how well do you know Tom Prado?"

"Who?"

"Tom Prado," Clint said. "One of the men who was chasing you on the beach."

"I don't know any of those men," she said. "I told you that. And I never heard of anyone named Tom Prado."

"That's what I thought."

"Are you comin' back inside?"

"First things first, Billie," he said. "Go into the house and stay close to Emily until I get back."

He walked down the steps and started around the lighthouse.

***

Initially, Clint had his doubts about leaving Emily and Billie in the house with Murrill and the other two men, but there were also some forty or so guests there. What could happen? Whatever Murrill wanted, he didn't want to shoot up a room full of people.

On the other hand, it seemed Marsh and his three friends would have no problem doing just that. So, as he had told Billie, first things first.

***

Murrill watched out a side window as Clint walked around to the beach.

"Wow," he said, loudly, "it looks like there's gonna be a gunfight down on the beach—four against one, but that one is the Gunsmith! Sounds like somethin' that should be seen."

"Certainly worth covering for the newspaper," the editor, Ferguson, said and ran out.

"I'm not missin' it," Peterson, the owner of the general store, said and also ran outside.

That started a virtual stampede of people leaving the house and running down to the beach.

***

When Clint reached the beach the four men were spread out across it. As he stepped onto the sand he heard sounds behind him, turned to see Ferguson, and then most of the party goers lining up. He saw Billie right out in front, watching and Emily standing next to her.

He didn't see Murrill, and his two friends.

That wasn't a good sign.

"Adams!" Marsh shouted.

Clint decided to get this over with quickly.

"I don't know what you're thinking, Marsh," he said, walking toward the four men, "but I don't have time for this."

"Sure you do," Marsh asked. "There's plenty of time to die."

"Looks like all you've got time for is talking," Clint said, still walking, "so just pull your guns and let's get it done."

"What's he doin'?" one of the other men said.

"Tell him ta stop walkin'," another said.

For a moment Marsh looked past Clint, searching for something.

"Adams!" Marsh yelled.

"Come on!" Clint shouted back.

Suddenly one of the other men—from fear or nerves—grabbed for his gun, and the others did the same.

Clint had no time to be fancy. These four had sealed their own fates. He drew and fired quickly, one, two, three, four times. Each man fell to the sand in turn, and he knew each man was dead. He walked to them to check anyway, just to make sure. As he walked back to the lighthouse he ejected his spent shells, reloaded the gun and holstered it.

"Adams," Ferguson, the newspaper editor said, "that was amazing. Can we—"

"No!"

"Mr. Adams," Chief Anderson said, "we need to talk."

"Later!"

Others were simply awed by what had happened and backed away to let him by.

When he reached Emily he grabbed her arm and said, "Come with me," and pulled her back to the lighthouse. Billie followed.

Once inside he closed the door, leaving everyone else on the outside.

"What's going on?"

"Everyone from the party was out on the beach, watching."

"Yes, so—"

"Except for the three men."

Her eyes widened.

"My God!" she looked around. "They're still here?"

"I doubt it," Clint said. "I'm sure they're gone. What I need you to tell me is, what did they take with them?"

Chapter Forty-Four

"Nothing's missing," Emily said.

Clint was looking out the front window. Most of the people had gone, some were still milling about. He was happy to see that both Ferguson and Chief Anderson had gone. The undertaker had also gone, taking the bodies of the four men with him.

He turned from the window to look at her. Billie was sitting on the sofa.

"And the gold?"

"Clint," Emily said, "there is no gold. There's never been any gold."

"Okay," he said. "Just checking."

"Do you want some coffee?"

"Yes."

Emily went into the kitchen.

"How do you feel?" Billie asked.

He looked at her, still distracted.

"What?"

"How do you feel?"

"About what?"

"Well . . . you killed four men less than an hour ago," she said. "I was just wondering what that feels like."

"It doesn't feel like anything."

"Really?"

He walked over and sat across from her.

"I used to feel sick after killing a man," he said, "but that went away years ago."

"So you don't feel happy?"

"Happy? Why would I feel happy?"

"That you're still alive."

"No," he said. "I'm glad I'm still alive, but I can't say I'm happy about what happened on the beach."

Emily came back in with three mugs—coffee for her and Clint, and tea for Billie. She sat next to the young girl.

"Well," she said, "that was some party."

"You didn't get what you wanted?" Billie asked.

"I think we got what we wanted," Clint said, "and they got what they wanted."

"What do you mean?" Emily asked.

"Murrill—that's the man I talked to upstairs—I'm sure that he somehow convinced those four men to call me out, assuring them that he and his two friends would help them."

"What makes you think that?" Emily asked.

"Two things," he said. "One, calling me out onto the beach, they succeeded in emptying the house, and two, at one point on the beach, Marsh looked past me. He was looking for Murrill and his two friends, expecting them to be there. But they weren't, because they were in here."

"Doing what?" Billie asked.

"That's what Emily has to tell us."

Emily looked at him over her mug and said, "I had some money and jewelry in my room. It's still there. Nothing is missing. Nothing of value, anyway."

"Then we need to go through the house and see if anything else is missing," he said.

"You mean . . . something of no value?" Emily asked.

"Of no value to you," Clint said, "but maybe of value to them."

"What could that be?" she asked.

"I don't know," Clint said.

"Well," Emily said, putting her mug down, "I guess we should start looking around again."

Clint and Billie put their mugs down, and they all stood up.

***

After half-an-hour Emily dropped her hands to her sides helplessly.

"I don't see a thing," she said.

"What about upstairs?"

"There's nothing of mine upstairs," she said. "Everything I value is down here."

"Yes, but they wouldn't know that, would they?"

"But what would they take-oh no!"

"What?"

"No!" she said again, and ran for the stairs.

"Emily! What is it?" Clint called. He ran after her, followed by Billie.

When they reached her she was standing in front of the light.

"Oh, no!" she cried.

"Emily?" Clint said.

She turned to him, her face pale and panicked.

"They took one of the lenses."

"Only one?" Clint asked. "Is that—"

"It can't work without all its components," she said.

"So that's what they wanted," Clint said. "The lens."

"But why?" Billie asked.

"Is it valuable?" Clint asked.

"Well, yes," Emily said. "The light can't work without it."

"Can it be replaced?"

"It would take forever," she said. "You can't just go into the general store and buy one."

"Then that's it," Clint said.

"What?" Billie asked.

"Now that they've got it," he said, "they can sell it back."

Chapter Forty-Five

"So they . . . kidnapped it?" Emily asked, later.

The three of them were sitting around the kitchen table, munching on food that was left from the party.

"You could say that," he said. "Tell me, how big is it?"

"It's about five inches wide, and seventeen inches tall," she said.

"So one of them could have carried it."

"But they'd have to be careful." she said. "If they break it—"

"If they break it they can't sell it back," he said.

"What if they don't wanna sell it back?" Billie asked.

"Then what would they want with it?" Clint asked.

"Well . . . maybe they want to sell it to someone else?" Billie offered.

"It's only use for it is the lighthouse," Emily said.

"Another lighthouse, maybe?" Billie asked.

Clint looked at Emily.

"Could another lighthouse keeper have hired them to steal it?"

"I doubt it," she said. "I just can't see it."

"I suppose I could go and have a look," Clint said. "I mean, at some of the other lighthouses, see if maybe their lights are out and if they need a lens like this one?"

"They're miles apart, Clint," Emily said. "I really don't think that's it." Her shoulders slumped. "I suppose I'll have to go to the police. Maybe they can catch those men before they leave town. They really can't just put the lens into one of their saddlebags."

"No," Clint said, "they'll need a buckboard or something, right?"

Emily nodded. "It's heavy," she said.

"All right," he said, "I'm going to head to town and see what I can find out."

"All right," Emily said, "but what about the police?"

"I can talk to them," Clint said. "And if the chief wants a statement from you, I'll have him send someone out here."

"Can I stay here?" Billie asked.

"I think you better go home, Billie," Clint said. "Your aunt will probably be worried."

"She doesn't care," Billie said.

"She does, Billie," Emily said. "Why do you think she came here with you today?"

"To make sure I didn't have . . . any fun," Billie said.

"I doubt that's it," Clint said.

"Will you take me back to town, then?" Billie asked him.

"Sure," he said, "let's go."

"Fine," Emily said, "leave me to clean this up all by myself."

Clint and Billie looked at her, then at each other.

"Oh, I'm just kidding, you two," Emily said. "Go. Finding the lens is more important."

"I can send the delivery back to help you," Clint said.

"Never mind! Just get out of here."

Clint took Billie's hand and led her to the leanto, where she waited for him to saddle Eclipse.

"Come on," he said. "Up you go."

"Can we ride together?" she asked.

"Not if we take your shortcut."

"Then let's go the long way," she said.

"Why not?" he said. "I doubt they're going to get very far lugging that lens."

He mounted up, then reached down for her hand and pulled her up behind him. She hiked her dress up so she could straddle the horses, then wrapped her arms around him and hugged herself to him. She had strong looking thighs.

"Let's go, Eclipse."

He shook the reins and off they went.

"Clint?" Billie said, her face pressed to his back.

"Yes?"

"Can we stop for a bit?"

"Billie—"

"Just a few minutes."

"All right."

He reined Eclipse to a stop and Billie slid down from behind him. As he watched, she pulled her dress down to cover her legs.

"What is it?" he asked.

"Can't you get down?"

He dismounted.

"Billie—"

Abruptly she hurled herself at him and kissed him. He stumbled back and they started to fall, so he put his arms around her to stop them. She took this to mean he was returning her kiss, so she opened her mouth. Abruptly, he put his hands on her hips and pushed her away.

"Billie, we talked about this!"

She looked down.

"I thought . . . if you kissed me . . . you'd change your mind."

"I'm sorry," he said, "but no."

"Well then," she asked, "how about this?"

She must have planned this, because as she pulled her dress over her head, he saw that she had no underwear on. She dropped the dress to the ground and was totally naked. Her body was more womanly than he would have thought. Wide hips, round, almost large breasts with pale nipples that were already hard. Her hair was almost red when it was clean, and she had the freckles of a redhead. The bush between her strong thighs was like burnished copper.

"Billie," he said, "you're a beautiful girl."

"Then will you make love to me?"

"No, I won't," he said.

"But I'm not a child!"

"You certainly don't look like a child," he admitted. "But you're seventeen, Billie. You're too young for me."

She stared at his crotch.

"It doesn't look like I'm too young for you," she said. She ran her hands over her breasts. "Are you sure?"

"I'm positive," he said. "Now put your dress back on and let's go."

Sulking, she pulled her dress back over her head. They mounted Eclipse and headed for town.

Chapter Forty-Six

When they got back, Clint dropped Billie off at the rooming house.

"What should I tell Aunt Janet?" she asked.

"Nothing," he said, as he lowered her to the ground, "and I mean nothing. Understand?"

She grinned at him and said, "I understand."

"Okay."

"Only . . ."

"Only what?"

"I could tell her we had sex."

"Billie—"

"Then she'd be mad at both of us."

"Billie, you can't—"

"Oh, relax," she said to him. "I'm not gonna tell her anythin'."

"I have to go and find that lens," he said.

"Then go," she said. "You have to help Emily."

"Stay in the house until I find those three, all right?" he said.

"Okay," she said. "It's nice that you worry about me."

"Go inside!"

She turned and ran to the door.

He turned Eclipse and rode toward the center of town.

***

"What are we gonna do with this now?" Prado asked.

Murrill went to the window of his hotel room and looked down at the street.

"We're supposed to hold it until our employer comes to get it," he said. "Then we get paid."

"So we ain't even gonna leave town?" Archer asked.

"No."

"But they're gonna be lookn' for us," Prado said. "The law."

"And Adams," Archer added.

Murrill turned to face them.

"They're gonna think we left town with it," he said. "They'd never think we'd stay. Who'd be that stupid?"

"Yeah," Prado wondered, "who?"

"And this employer?" Archer asked. "Are we gonna find out who it is?"

"Up to now it hasn't been necessary," Murrill pointed out, "but yeah, you probably will."

"So what do we do in the meantime?" Prado asked.

"We stay here," Murrill said.

"In this flea trap of a hotel?" Archer asked. "The worst place in town?"

"Yes," Murrill said, "in this place."

"For how long?" Prado asked.

Murrill turned back to the window.

"We'll have to wait and see."

***

Clint checked every livery stable in town. Nobody had rented a buckboard or a buggy. He knew that Murrill and his men had horses. But to transport the lens they'd need to rent something.

They had not yet left town.

Clint rode to the Whiskey Station and walked in. There were several men there, but as soon as they saw him they walked out.

"Something I said?" he asked the bartender.

"Somethin' you did," the man said. "Words got out you killed Marsh and those other three on the beach in a clean gunfight."

"And now I'm looking for the other three," Clint said.

"To kill them, too?'

"No," Clint said, "but they put Marsh and his bunch up to facing me, while they stole something out of the lighthouse."

The bartender thought about that for a minute, then said with raised eyebrows, "Hey, that's kinda smart."

"Yes, it was," Clint said. "Thanks."

"For what?" the bartender asked. "I didn't say anything."

"Yes," Clint said, "actually you did."

Chapter Forty-Seven

Clint rode from the Whiskey Saloon over to the Beach Grove Saloon. He expected to get more information from Jim the bartender than from anyone else. And he didn't like Chief Anderson, which was why he was leaving the police as a last resort.

It was dark by the time he reached his goal. He entered and—as had happened at the Whiskey—the men who were drinking there decided they'd better do it somewhere else. There was almost a line going out the front door, and by the time the exodus was over there were three men who chose their whiskey over leaving.

As Clint approached the bar Jim spread his hands.

"Thanks for clearin' me out."

"Do they really think I'm going to shoot them?" Clint asked.

"Did Marsh and his partners think you were gonna shoot them?"

"They brought that on themselves."

"Beer?"

"Why not?"

Jim set it in front of him.

"What's on your mind?"

"Money," Clint said.

"You have some, or you're lookin' for some?"

"I'm looking for some," Clint said. "That is, I'm looking for somebody with a lot of it."

"Well," Jim said, "you played poker with the people who have the most money in town."

"Those people?" Clint asked. "The chief-of-police?"

"Anderson?" Jim said. "He was rich way before they made him chief. In fact, most people think he bought the position."

"I thought I was playing with storekeepers."

"You were," Jim said, "storekeepers with money."

"And the lawyer? Barrett?"

"Mmm, well, he gets paid to represent the people with the money."

"And what about Janet Evans?"

"Her?" Jim rolled his eyes. "She might have the most money of all."

"Are you serious?"

"Dead serious. The lady is loaded."

Clint frowned.

"Problem?"

"I think so," Clint said. "You know a man named Murrill—Mitch Murrill?"

"Nope, can't say I do. He one of the ones you're lookin' for?"

"Yep, him and his two friends."

"Well, if they're not from here, I wouldn't know them. And if they're strangers, they've stayed out of here. You'd probably find out more at the Whiskey."

"Yeah, I thought that, too. Let me ask you something else."

"Go ahead," Jim said. "Doesn't look like I'm gonna have too many customers while you're here."

"I'll be gone in a minute," Clint said. "You didn't come to the party."

"Yeah, I'm not the party type."

"I saw the way the women looked at Emily Fish, the lighthouse keeper."

"Oh yeah," Jim said, "they don't think much of her. Now the men . . ."

"Yeah, I saw that, too," Clint said. "Look, just between you and me, somebody stole a lens piece. Without it the light doesn't work."

"That's not good."

"I've been trying to figure out why somebody would want to do that," Clint told him. "It's not like they could sell it easily."

"So what do you think happened?"

"With a bunch like that, they'd only do something if they knew they were going to make money."

"You mean, like if they were bein' paid?"

"Exactly."

"So who would pay them?"

"Somebody who doesn't like Emily Fish," Clint said. "Somebody who wants her to lose her job."

"So another woman, then?"

Clint nodded. "A woman with money."

"Uh-oh," Jim said, "I think I know who we're talkin' about."

"I'll have to check."

"What about the police?"

"I don't want to get her in trouble," Clint said. "I just want to find out where the lens is, and get it back to the lighthouse."

"Well, if that means you're gonna leave my saloon so I can make some money, I'm all for it," Jim said, with a smile.

Clint finished his beer and said, "You're all heart."

"Come on back when you're done," Jim called, as Clint went out the batwings, "and everyone's forgot what you did."

Chapter Forty-Eight

Clint thought he might be jumping to a conclusion, but he had to find out for sure. He rode Eclipse over to the rooming house, let himself in through the unlocked front door.

Janet Evans turned to face him in the livingroom, frowning.

"You don't have a room here, anymore," she said. "What do you want?"

"I came to talk to you," Clint said.

"Why?"

"I've been trying to figure out who would want to do something to hurt the lighthouse, to hurt Emily."

"And you decided it was me?" she asked.

"I decided it was somebody who doesn't like her, who has the money to pay three men to steal the lens from the lighthouse."

"Again," she said, folding her arms, "you came up with me."

"Well," he admitted, "I came up with you first."

"What makes you think I have the money to hire three idiots to steal anything?" she demanded, waving her arms. "You see how empty this place is."

"I know," he said, "I also don't see you doing anything to try and change things. I can only figure you don't need the money this place might bring in."

"Anything else?"

"Well, the poker game," he said. "You play poker regularly with the wealthy men in town, and from what I saw, you win."

"They're idiots," she said. "They don't expect me to win, so I do."

"Come on, Janet," Clint said. "It was you, right? You've got something against her, and you set this up."

She kept her arms folded and stared at him, but she didn't deny it. Neither did she confirm it.

"Aunt Janet?"

She turned her head quickly, looked at Billie standing on the stairs.

"Is this true?" Billie asked. "You did it to hurt Emily?"

"Billie . . . you shouldn't be seeing her . . ."

"She's my friend."

"She's a harlot."

"What are you talking about?"

"Did you know her before she came here?" Clint asked. "Or for that matter, before you came here?"

"Let's just say we have a past," Janet said, "and I know the real Emily Fish. She's a bitch!"

"So you hired three men to sabotage her lighthouse? Get her fired?"

"Hopefully," she said.

"Well," he said, "it's not going to happen. I need you to tell me where those men are. Murrill and his boys. And the lens."

"And why would I do that?" Janet asked. "You'll just take it back to her—and probably have sex with her."

"That's none of your business, Janet," Clint said.

Billie came down the stairs and confronted her aunt.

"Tell him, Aunt Janet! Tell him where it is."

Janet looked away.

"All right, then," Clint said, "let's go to the police."

"What?" Janet asked.

"I'm turning you in."

"You can't prove anything."

"Yes, he can," Billie said. "I'm a witness."

"Billie!"

"You better tell him!"

Janet unfolded her arms and glared at the both of them.

"Fine," she said. "There's a hotel over the deadline . . ."

***

"Are you sure she's gonna meet us here?" Prado asked.

"That's what she said," Murrill said.

"I can't believe it's the rooming house lady," Archer said. "Why would she want this lens?"

"She's got it in for the lighthouse keeper, for some reason," Murrill said. "When she found me in the saloon and offered me the money, I said yes."

"She came to the Whiskey?" Archer asked. "Her?"

"No," Murrill said, "one of the other ones. She made the offer, and I said yes for the three of us."

"So we get our final payment tonight and get out of town tomorrow?" Prado asked.

"Exactly."

"If she'd just get here," Archer said. "Otherwise, what the hell are we supposed to do with that."

They all looked at the lens standing in the corner of the room.

"She'll be here," Murrill said.

At that moment there was a knock at the door.

"See?" Murrill asked. "What did I tell you?"

He walked to the door and opened it, staggered back as Clint pushed him and entered, his gun in his hand.

"Gentlemen," he said.

"Jesus!" Prado said.

"Anyone goes for their gun you know what's going to happen," Clint said.

"What do you want?" Murrill demanded.

"That," Clint said, indicating the lens in the corner with the barrel of his gun. "Now, you fellas are all going to drop your gunbelts, and then we're going to take that back where it belongs."

"No, we ain't," Murrill said.

"We're going to take it back," Clint said, "or we're going to take it to the police station. It's your choice."

The three men exchanged glances, and then un-strapped their guns and let them drop to the floor.

Chapter Forty-Nine

The next morning Clint woke with Emily's impressive fanny pressed up against his crotch, as he lay spooned behind her. Immediately, his cock began to stiffen. He slid it along the crease between her butt cheeks until she woke, and spread her legs so he could enter her from behind . . .

***

"You saved me, you know," she told him at breakfast. "You kept me from having even one dark night in the lighthouse. I'll never forget you for that."

"That's all you'll never forget me for?" he asked.

She just smiled at him and put another flapjack on his plate.

"Are you really leaving today?" she asked.

"I am," he said, "right from here."

"What about those three men?"

"If they're lucky they left last night, in the dark," he said. "I told them if I saw them again, I'd turn them over to the police."

"And Janet?"

"Billie told her she'd turn her in if she bothered you again."

"Billie said that?"

"Yes."

"She's a sweet girl."

"But before I go," he said, "why don't you tell me what happened between you and Janet Evans?"

"It happened a long time ago," she said, "far away from here. Two girls, one man . . . isn't it always a man? And when we ran into each other here I realized she'd never forgiven me . . . I think that's why she treats Billie so bad."

"Maybe they'll talk it out," Clint said. "Or maybe not. I can't stay around to find out."

"I'll talk with Billie," Emily said. "Maybe I can get her to take it easy on her aunt."

"I hope so."

***

Later she walked him outside and watched as he saddled Eclipse, and then mounted up.

"If you're ever in the neighborhood."

"Count on it."

She reached out and they clasped hands briefly before he urged Eclipse on. About a hundred yards later he turned and took his last look at the lighthouse at Point Pinos.

Now Available!

AWARD-WINNING AUTHOR
ROBERT J. RANDISI
TALBOT ROPER NOVELS

For more information
visit: www.SpeakingVolumes.us

Now Available!

ROBERT J. RANDISI'S
RAT PACK MYSTERIES

GET SWEPT AWAY INTO
THE LAS VEGAS ERA OF THE 60s

For more information
visit: www.SpeakingVolumes.us